A waiter arrived and started mopping at the puddle on the tablecloth in front of me with a rag. I didn't look up at first, so I didn't see his face. As he continued wiping I saw that some of the liquid was headed straight for my lap.

"Watch out!" I cried.

"Sorry about that," he said in a low voice.

I turned to face him for the first time—and looked straight into a pair of the biggest, deepest brown eyes I'd ever seen. I caught my breath. It was as if those eyes, looking directly at me through those thick, dark lashes, could actually *speak* to me—as if they were communicating directly with something deep inside me.

Suddenly I couldn't move. Couldn't speak, couldn't do anything. The rest of the world had disappeared. The restaurant and everybody in it had faded into the background, and the two of us were frozen in place.

Don't miss any of the books in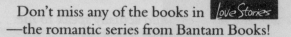
—the romantic series from Bantam Books!

*Love Stories*

# He's NOT
# What
# You
# Think

## Randi Reisfeld

BANTAM BOOKS
NEW YORK · TORONTO · LONDON · SYDNEY · AUCKLAND

RL 6, age 12 and up

HE'S NOT WHAT YOU THINK
*A Bantam Book / September 1997*

*Produced by Daniel Weiss Associates, Inc.*
*33 West 17th Street*
*New York, NY 10011.*
*Cover photography by Michael Segal.*

ISBN: 0-553-57077-3

*Published simultaneously in the United States and Canada*

*Bantam Books are published by Bantam Books, a division of Bantam*
*Doubleday Dell Publishing Group, Inc. Its trademark, consisting of the*
*words "Bantam Books" and the portrayal of a rooster, is Registered in*
*U.S. Patent and Trademark Office and in other countries. Marca*
*Registrada. Bantam Books, 1540 Broadway, New York, New York 10036.*

PRINTED IN THE UNITED STATES OF AMERICA

OPM     0 9 8 7 6 5 4 3 2 1

# ONE

I COULD FEEL the hot Florida sun beating down on my back as my best friend, Cami, and I stood together in the middle of the Lincoln Road outdoor mall.

Cami pushed her rhinestone-studded black sunglasses up onto her head of blond ringlets and sighed. The sun glinted off her small silver nose ring. "I'm broiling, Jess. And starving too. Can't we give it up and get a shake or something?"

"In a little while, okay?" I pleaded. "I don't want to stop until I've found the perfect bathing suit."

Lincoln Road Mall is the hottest shopping spot in South Beach, the area of Miami where Cami and I live. Cami and I had already been to about five swimwear boutiques, but I hadn't found anything I liked. Correction: I hadn't found anything I liked *enough*. You see, this wasn't just *any* bathing suit we were shopping for. If that were the case, one of the six million bathing suits I already had at home probably would have been fine. No, this was important. *This* was the bathing suit that was supposed to knock Jeremy Baer off his feet.

Cami sighed dramatically, then clutched at her throat and stuck out her tongue. She looked like somebody from an old movie crawling through the desert toward a mirage.

"Frappuccino . . . ," she gasped hoarsely, "must find frozen frappuccino . . ." She sank to her knees right there in the middle of the mall and put her hand to her forehead.

I sighed and shook my head. Cami's always doing stuff like that. It's like it's some kind of *requirement* for her to make a scene in a public place. Her dad's a psychiatrist, and Cami says that he thinks she seeks attention to confirm her self-worth and boost her self-esteem. Whatever. All I know is, if *I* looked like Camryn Welch, *my* self-esteem sure wouldn't need any help.

People in the mall were starting to stare. An old woman with an even older-looking gray poodle had stopped in her tracks. The woman's eyes were glued to Cami, and her mouth was hanging open.

Cami rolled her green eyes up toward me pleadingly. "I feel faint. . . . Jess, you've got to help me. . . . If I look at one more bikini, it could be the end for me. . . ."

I laughed. I nudged one of Cami's black vinyl boots with the toe of my clog. "Maybe if you didn't

2

have these dumb things on, you wouldn't be so hot," I pointed out. "It's ninety degrees today, and it must be at least a hundred and twenty inside those boots."

Cami wrinkled her forehead. "Hey, I love my boots." She stood up. "Besides, they look so great with this pink miniskirt." Then she noticed the old lady, who was still staring. "Hi!" Cami called out to her. "Cute dog. Can I have it?"

The woman scowled and hurried away.

I burst out laughing. "Cami, stop!"

"What?" Cami turned to me. "I think it liked me." Suddenly she stared off over my shoulder and her eyes widened. "Hey, Jess, it's Jeremy! He just went into Scoops and Stuff!"

For a moment my throat tightened and my legs got all shaky, the way they always did when Jeremy was around.

Then I got hold of myself. "Oh, yeah, right," I said to Cami. "Nice try. All right, look, if you really want to get a shake that badly—"

"Jess, I'm not kidding!" Cami insisted. "Jeremy just walked into Scoops and Stuff with Halcy and two guys from school."

I whipped around. "He's really in the ice-cream place?"

Cami grabbed my arm. "Come on, let's go."

I shook her off. "Okay, just wait a minute. I'm not sure if I'm ready."

After all, we were talking about Jeremy Baer, who was, as far as I was concerned, the major crush-worthy hunk of South Beach High. I had just spent an entire semester sitting two seats away from Jeremy in English class, trying to think of ways to start conversations with him. It wasn't as easy as you'd think, inventing reasons to borrow a pencil from someone who's two seats to your left. It was starting to seem completely hopeless, like I was doomed to gaze longingly at Jeremy's curly black hair and broad shoulders from the corner of my left eye forever.

Luckily last week, right before school let out for summer vacation, Cami had found out about the Bahamas cruise from Haley Patterson. Cami and Haley aren't really close friends, but their parents have known each other forever and belong to the same beach club. And Haley *is* really good friends with Mia Payne, who's the girlfriend of Mark Revis, who just so happens to be one of Jeremy's best friends. Anyway, Haley told Cami that she and Mark and Jeremy and Mia and a bunch of other kids from school were all booking spaces on this cruise to the Bahamas for the Fourth of July weekend. The Bahamas are really close to where we live. So Cami said maybe she'd go too, and maybe she'd bring another friend—which, of course, just happened to be me.

So now it was all worked out—all except the part where I asked my mom if I could go, that is. My mom's not too big on unchaperoned overnight activities. Also, she'd been in kind of a bad mood for a while—actually for about the last year or so, ever since my dad left us for Janie, this woman from his law firm, and moved to New York with her. Not that I can blame my mom. I mean, what my dad did was pretty terrible.

Anyway, here I was standing outside Scoops and Stuff, breaking out in a sweat knowing that Jeremy was inside and that I'd been shopping all afternoon for a bathing suit that was supposed to make him notice me on this cruise to the Bahamas that he probably still had no idea I was even going on. *If* he even knew who I was.

Cami grabbed me again. "Come on, Jess! You don't want to miss him, do you?" She pulled me toward the door to the ice-cream shop.

I took a quick inventory. What was I wearing? White tank top, plaid short-shorts, clogs. Not too bad. Could be better. Probably not what I would have picked out if I'd *known* I was going to see Jeremy today, but okay.

As we walked through the door Cami reached up and tugged out the white scrunchie that was holding up my hair, sending my auburn hair tumbling down my back.

I turned to her and glared. "What did you do that for?" I whispered.

"Looks better that way," Cami assured me. She stuck my scrunchie in my back pocket and pushed me into the store. "Oh, Haley!" she called, waving. "Hi! I didn't know you guys were in here."

I breathed deeply and tried to get my legs to stop shaking. There he was. There was Jeremy, sitting at a round table across from the counter with Haley, Mark Revis, and another guy I recognized from school but didn't really know. Jeremy was wearing a navy blue T-shirt and dark sunglasses, and he was eating some kind of green ice cream on a cone. He looked incredibly cute as usual.

As I walked toward the counter and the table where Jeremy was sitting, I suddenly felt like I had no idea what to do with my face. I tried to smile casually, like a girl who has just run into some people from school. The problem is it's almost impossible to smile casually on purpose. I'm sure I probably ended up looking more like some kind of crazed clown.

I sneaked a peek at Jeremy, my heart racing. He might have been looking at me, but it was hard to tell with his sunglasses on. It was also possible that he was looking at the Have Your Birthday at Scoops and Stuff cardboard display on the counter next to me.

"Try the white chocolate chip," Haley advised. "It's amazing."

"Maybe another time," Cami responded. "I already promised myself a frappuccino. What are you having, Jess?"

"Having?"

Cami nudged me hard. "Yeah. As in—we came in here to get ice cream, remember?"

I could feel my face getting hot. I turned toward the counter so Jeremy wouldn't see me blushing. Why did I always feel like such a total idiot around him? It was like the sight of him made me forget how to function or something. "Um, I'm not sure yet," I managed to mumble.

"One frappuccino, please," Cami informed the man behind the counter.

I pretended to study the menu board posted on the wall. *Turn back around and think of something to say to him,* I commanded myself. *This is your chance. You've been waiting all semester for this.*

"Hey, Cami, are you really going on the July Fourth cruise?" asked Haley.

"Sure," Cami replied. She reached for her frappuccino. "Sounds fun." She nudged me. "Jess is coming too."

"Cool," said a guy's voice. I strained to listen. Was that Jeremy? Or had it been the other guy? I felt like kicking myself. What was I doing with my back to everyone like this? Why hadn't I just ordered something right away? Then I could actually be taking part in this conversation!

I quickly scanned the menu board. I had to just pick something. Anything. But the only thing I seemed to be able to focus on was the Banana Boat Blast for $6.50, which was supposed to feed four to six people. That seemed a little excessive, especially since I wasn't even hungry.

"The mint chocolate chip is pretty good," said a deep voice behind me.

I whirled around and saw Jeremy standing inches away. He had taken off his sunglasses, and he was just finishing his cone.

"Oh, okay, thanks," I stammered. I turned to the man behind the counter. "I'll have a mint chocolate chip cone." *What am I doing?* I wondered. *I don't even like mint chocolate chip.*

"Good choice," Jeremy said, a twinkle in his dark blue eyes. He seemed to study me for a moment. "Hey, we have a class together, right?"

"English." I nodded. "With Mrs. Harkin," I added.

*Oh, that was bright,* I told myself—*like he might not know who his own English teacher is.*

"Oh, yeah." He put out his hand. "I'm Jeremy."

I slipped my hand into his. "Jessica."

He was still holding on to my hand. "So you're going to the Bahamas for the Fourth too, huh."

I nodded. His hand was warm and dry, and I wanted it to hold mine forever. "It sounds like it's going to be a really fun trip," I managed, trying to keep my voice from squeaking.

"Yeah, I bet." Jeremy gave my hand a quick squeeze, then dropped it. He turned to his friends at the table. "Come on, you guys. Let's get going. I want to make that flick at three o'clock." He turned back to me and winked. "Catch you on the cruise."

I felt like I was frozen in place. I stared after him as he, Haley, and the other guy made their way out of the shop.

Cami ambled over, slurping the end of her shake. "Hey, he talked to you, huh? How'd it go?"

I was still numb. "Good. Great, I think. I mean,

he winked at me. And he squeezed my hand too."

Cami raised her eyebrows. "Wow, sounds like if he'd stayed here any longer, you two would have started making out."

I stared out the window of the shop, wondering what movie Jeremy was going to see and where. Not that I ever would have asked him—being around Jeremy hadn't turned me into *that* much of a social misfit. But I couldn't help feeling envious of Haley and the other guy—and of the whole movie audience, in fact—because they were all about to spend two hours in the dark with Jeremy. Right now I couldn't think of anyplace I'd rather be.

I turned to Cami. "Cami, he remembered me from English, and he said he'd see me on the cruise!" I seized her arm. "Come on, we have to get going right away! I have to get a bathing suit for this trip immediately!"

"Hold on! Hold on!" Cami was laughing. "Aren't you forgetting something, Jess?"

"What?"

She pointed to the counter. My mint chocolate chip ice-cream cone was sitting in the little metal stand there, waiting for me to pick it up. It was melting pretty heavily, and the green ice cream had begun to drip on the counter.

"Forget it, I don't want it," I replied quickly. I glanced at the man behind the counter, who was giving me a pretty nasty look.

"Oh, don't be such a sourpuss," Cami told him. She dug into the pocket of her skirt and fished out a crumpled-up bill. "Here, just take this!" she said, throwing the money on the counter.

Just then I spotted something on the table where Jeremy and the others had been sitting.

"Oh, wow, Jeremy left his sunglasses!" I hurried over and picked them up. They were pretty ordinary sunglasses, the same kind of black Ray-Bans that lots of the kids at school wear, but somehow picking them up felt almost like I was holding a little piece of Jeremy in my hand.

I put the sunglasses on.

"I hate to tell you this, Jess," said Cami. "But those are absolutely the wrong shape for your face."

I shrugged. "I know." I took the sunglasses off. Then I did something really cheesy—so cheesy, I almost hate to admit it. I kissed them.

Cami started laughing. "And people call *me* weird."

I laughed too. I knew it was weird, but I couldn't help it. I had been thinking about Jeremy and trying to get him to notice me for so long. I couldn't believe that today we had finally had a real conversation!

Everything was finally going my way. Now I only had to do three things—find a bathing suit, convince my mom to let me go on the cruise, and make it till the Fourth without going absolutely crazy!

# TWO

L ATER THAT EVENING I stood in the kitchen, staring into the refrigerator, wondering for about the millionth time where my mother was. It was pretty unusual for her not to be home at five o'clock. Actually, lately it was pretty unusual for her not to be home *all* the time. Like I said, she'd been kind of down for a while, ever since my dad left, and she hadn't been going out and doing a lot of the stuff she used to.

When my parents were still together, even though my mom didn't have a job, she was very busy. She took aerobics classes at her gym, and she volunteered as a tutor once a week at an elementary school in downtown Miami. She was always going places with her friends. But not anymore. I worried about her sometimes. Old people like to talk about the good old days, when moms stayed home to be with their kids. But I can say from firsthand experience that it's definitely not all it's cracked up to be—especially if your mom's

11

staying home because she's too depressed to go out.

I closed the refrigerator and opened a cabinet. I'd been munching nonstop since I got home from the mall. I always eat when I'm worked up about something or excited. And right then, thanks to Jeremy Baer and his wink, I had already devoured a peanut butter sandwich, half a bag of pretzels, and an orange. I knew I'd better slow down a little soon, though. I couldn't just eat my way to July Fourth. At least, not if I planned on fitting into my new bathing suit.

I had finally found a great suit in this store called Splash. It was just a simple white bikini, but it fit absolutely perfectly. Cami had agreed right away that it was the one. It was a little expensive but definitely worth it.

Cami had bought a suit too—a bright orange thong bikini with a top that looked like it was made out of a couple of postage stamps and a few pieces of string. I never could have worn something like that on the beach in a million years without dying of embarrassment. But *embarrassment* was a word that wasn't part of Cami's vocabulary. Besides, she looked incredible in it.

After we'd finished shopping Cami had said she wanted to go over to Bodywerx and have her belly button pierced. Her mother had signed the parental permission form, and Cami was carrying it in her bag. She asked me to go with her, but I said no. I had already gone to Bodywerx once with Cami, when she had her nose pierced, and that was enough for me. There was no way I wanted to watch somebody stick one of those big needles into her stomach.

I grabbed a bag of oatmeal cookies and closed the cabinet. I heard my mother's car pull into the driveway. A moment later she came through the side door into the kitchen.

"Hi, sweetie," she said with a smile. "I hope you weren't worried. I expected to be home earlier."

"Hi, Mom." I took a bite of an oatmeal cookie. "Where were you anyway?" I asked, my mouth full of crumbs.

"Wait till I tell you." Her face lit up even more. I hadn't seen my mom look this happy in a long time. Her cheeks were pink, and her blue eyes were sparkling. This was good. This was probably going to make it a lot easier to talk to her about the cruise.

"Tell me what?" I asked.

"Jess, I've got great news," she said. "At least, it's great news as far as I'm concerned, and I hope you'll be as happy about it as I am."

My heart leaped. For a moment I thought that maybe she was going to tell me that my dad had decided to come back. He was leaving Janie and New York and rejoining the family.

*Don't be stupid,* I told myself. *Stuff like that never happens in real life.* I pushed the thought out of my mind, shoved it into some tiny closet in my brain, and slammed a door on it.

"Well, sweetheart, I've decided to go back to work," my mother announced happily.

"Back?" I repeated. "What are you talking about, Mom? You never worked."

"Sure, I did," she said a little defensively. "Before you were born. When I met your father. I was a teacher's aide."

"Oh, that, right." I took another bite of cookie. "Um, no offense, Mom, but aren't you a little old for a job like that? I mean, aren't most teacher's aides college students or something?"

My mother waved her hand. "Oh, honey, I'm not going to get another job as an aide. This time I'm going to be a teacher."

"Oh," I said. "That sounds good. But can you just *decide* to be a teacher, just like that?" Teachers always seemed like they were some separate species to me. It was hard to imagine that my mother could just turn into one one day.

"I've got it all worked out," she answered. "It turns out that most of my old credits from Boston College will transfer, and there are just a couple of courses more I've got to take to get my Florida teacher's license."

"Courses?" I repeated. "You mean like college courses?"

She nodded. "That's right. Luckily for me there's an excellent summer program up in Pensacola where I can get it all done at once. I might even be able to get a teaching job by fall."

Now I was having trouble processing. Suddenly what she was saying didn't seem to be making sense anymore. "Summer program? In Pensacola? But that's hours away from here. You can't take classes there, Mom."

She smiled. "I can if I stay in a dorm!"

14

"What?" I stared at her. "Stay in a dorm? With a bunch of college kids? Are you kidding?"

"Oh, Jess, really," my mother said. "They won't exactly be *kids*. This is an advanced program, after all."

"Yeah, but don't you think you'll be just a little bit more *advanced* than everyone else?" I asked.

She looked hurt.

I felt bad. "I'm sorry, Mom. I guess I'm just surprised. I think it's great you want to go do something for yourself like that." Then I thought of something. "But what about me? What am I supposed to do while you're off at college?"

My mother paused. "Well, the course is only for a month. I've thought of a solution for that too."

A solution? What was I suddenly, some kind of problem my mom felt like she had to solve? I waited to hear what she would say. Maybe she'd tell me that I was on my own for a month for the summer, that I could do whatever I wanted. Somehow I doubted it, but it would be nice.

My mother forced a smile. "You're going to spend some time with your father," she said lightly. "He's decided to take a vacation up in a mountain resort in the Catskills, a couple of hours outside of New York City, and he wants you to spend the month there too."

"You mean with *Janie?*" I stared at her in amazement. My mom and I didn't talk about it too much, but I was pretty sure we both felt exactly the same way about my father's new girlfriend. I had only met Janie once, at a restaurant about six months ago. My dad was in Miami on business, and it was supposed to be just the two of us meeting for lunch. But at the last minute he'd brought Janie along on the trip too, so she showed up at the restaurant with him.

It was a terrible meal. I couldn't stand Janie from the moment I met her. She was dressed in a pale blue suit that made her look like a flight attendant, and she sent her chicken back to the chef twice because she didn't like the way it was cooked. I couldn't believe my dad had left my mom for her. Meanwhile my father was putting all this energy into acting upbeat and happy, like the three of us were some cozy little family. But all I could think about was that this obnoxious woman was my mom's replacement. I was so angry at both of them that I hardly said a word. My dad hadn't tried anything like that again.

"Why, yes, she'll be there too, I assume," my mother responded. "After all, your father will probably be married to her one day." She exhaled deeply. "Jess, I think this time with your father could be good for you—"

"You mean good for *you!*" I shot back.

"Jess, please—"

I shook my head. "Forget it. I'm not going." I thought about Jeremy and the cruise. I thought about my bathing suit, still in the bag from Splash, upstairs on my bed. "Just tell Dad I said no."

My mother fixed her eyes on mine. "I can't do that," she said in a low voice. "Jessie, you are not the only person involved here. Going back to school to get my license is very important to me."

16

"Well, did you ever stop to think about what might be important to *me*?" I demanded. Suddenly there were tears in my eyes. "What about my friends? What about Cami?"

Right away I knew mentioning Cami was a mistake. My mother had never been crazy about Cami. She was probably *happy* about the idea of my being separated from Cami for the summer.

My mother sighed. "You and Camryn Welch have spent practically every waking moment together for the entire school year. I think you'll survive a month apart, Jess. And your father is really looking forward to spending some time with you."

I scowled. If he wanted to spend so much time with me, why did he get together with Janie and move out of town?

My mother's tone got businesslike. "It's all settled. I registered for the Pensacola program today, and your father's booking a flight for you next week."

Next week? Then I was going to miss the Bahamas cruise for sure! And from the way my mother was talking, there was absolutely nothing I could do about it.

"Oh, great!" I yelled, tears spilling from my eyes. "Thanks a lot for messing up my whole life, Mom!"

"Please, there's no need to get so dramatic, Jess," said my mother. "It's not your whole life. It's only for part of the summer. Besides, I'm sure you'll have a lot better time up north than you think."

But I knew there was no way that was true. This cruise was going to be my chance with Jeremy—my chance at first love. And now it was ruined!

# THREE

"MAYBE IT WON'T be so bad up there," Cami ventured.

I looked at her. "Cami, please. Golden's Resort Hotel in Beaverkill, New York? How good can it be?"

Cami made a face. "Beaverkill, huh?"

I nodded.

Cami lay back on my bed and stared up at the ceiling, her feet dangling over the edge of the bed. "Sounds pretty nowhere," she admitted.

"Besides, it doesn't even matter where it is. The point is that I have to be *here*, to go on that cruise," I reminded her. I shifted in my seat, an antique rocking chair in the corner of my room.

"The cruise isn't such a big deal, believe me," Cami replied. "I've been to the Bahamas three times. It's basically just beaches."

"Beaches with Jeremy Baer on them," I pointed

out. I sighed. "Look, Cami, I know this might be hard for you to understand, since you can get practically any boy in the world just by snapping your fingers—"

"That's not true!" Cami objected. She snickered. "Sometimes I have to clap too."

I laughed. That's one thing I appreciate about Cami—she's never fake. I mean, if you're going to have a best friend who's simultaneously totally out of her mind, incredibly rich, and completely irresistible to guys, it helps somehow if she admits it all.

"Anyway, for those of us who live in the real world, it isn't always so easy," I finished.

"Believe me, it's not so great for me either," said Cami. "Most of the guys I go out with end up being total bores." She sat up and grimaced a little in pain.

"Belly button?" I asked.

She nodded. "It's only supposed to hurt for a few days. The swelling will go down soon too. Want to see?" She started to unbutton the purple Smurf pajama top she was wearing as a shirt.

I made a face. "No, thanks."

"Anyway, I see your point about Jeremy. You don't want to give up your big chance to lock lips with something more than his sunglasses." She shrugged. "So I guess we just have to figure out a way to get you out of this trip to the mountains."

"Forget it." I sighed. "My mom is totally set on this."

"What about your dad?" asked Cami. "Have you talked to him about it yet?"

I shook my head. "No, but my mother said everything's arranged with him too. He's probably buying my plane ticket right now."

"Talk to your father," Cami suggested. "Tell him you think it's crucial for your social development to be with your peer group right now. That kind of stuff works on my dad all the time."

"Yeah, well, my dad's not a psychiatrist," I reminded her. "He's a lawyer."

Cami bit her lip. "I guess there isn't any *legal* reason we can come up with why you couldn't go?"

I laughed. "You mean like I can't cross the state line because I'm wanted? I don't think so." I groaned. "Oh, Cami, what am I going to do?" I stood up and walked over to my oak bureau. Jeremy's sunglasses were lying on top of it, and I picked them up. "A whole month without seeing him—or you either! I feel like I'm being sentenced to jail!"

"Believe me, I'm not exactly thrilled about spending a month here without you," Cami replied. "It's going to be beyond boring."

The phone rang.

Cami reached over to my night table and picked it up. "Ms. Jessica Graham's private line. This is her secretary speaking. How may I help you, please?" She paused a moment. "Oh, okay, hang on a second." She put her hand over the receiver. "It's your father," she told me. "Just tell him you don't want to go!" she added in a whisper.

It sounded so simple when Cami put it that way.

But that was because Cami's parents let her do whatever she wanted. Her father had some theory that it would stunt Cami's development if she didn't make all her own decisions. And her mom was too busy running her interior design business to care.

I took a deep breath as she handed me the phone. "Hi, Dad."

"Well, hello, there, Jess!" His voice was loud and cheerful. "Glad I caught you at home." He chuckled. "Sounds like you're a busy executive these days."

"That was just a friend of mine," I explained. I made a face at Cami. "A friend who doesn't know how to answer a telephone like a normal person."

He laughed. "Listen, I just wanted to let you know that I booked you a flight for next Wednesday. Two P.M. Janie and I will meet you at JFK here in New York, and we can all drive up to the mountains together."

"Actually, Dad, I kind of wanted to talk to you about—" I began.

"What's that?" He cut me off. "Hold on, honey. Janie wants to say a few words."

Before I could object, Janie's voice came on the line. "Jessica? Janie Baxter here. Listen, I just wanted to let you know how pleased I am that you'll be joining us, dear."

I gritted my teeth. Even over the phone Janie seemed like such a phony.

"It means the world to your father," Janie went on. "He misses you so very much."

21

I desperately wanted to hang up on her. I hated the way she talked about my father, as though she'd known him for a million years.

"Put my father back on the phone, please," I told her curtly.

"Oh, all right, dear. Just a moment. Here he is."

My father's voice came back on the line. "Honey? Hi. Listen, it's like Janie said, we're really looking forward to this."

"Actually, Dad, I'm not really sure I can go," I told him.

"What?" he said. "Why? What's happening? Don't tell me your mother changed her mind. Not after I've gone ahead and made the reservations! If that's the case, Jess, you just let me talk to her—"

"No, no, Dad, that's not it," I interrupted. I paused. "*I'm* the one who doesn't want to go."

"But Jess . . ." His voice sounded hurt. "Listen, honey, I think you're going to have the time of your life. Golden's Resort has everything—a pool, tennis, horseback riding. There's even a disco!"

"It sounds great, Dad," I lied. "But I really want to be with my friends this summer. My friend Cami and I, we have a lot of plans." I glanced at Cami, and she nodded encouragingly.

"Cami? Who's she? I don't think I know her," said my father.

"She's the one who answered the phone. I think you met her a couple of times last year," I told him. "Anyway, she's kind of like my best friend now, and we both—"

22

"Terrific!" he boomed. "Tell you what, Jess, bring her along!"

"Bring her?" I repeated in astonishment. "You mean to the Catskills with us?"

"Sure, why not?" answered my dad. "You two girls will have a ball here. Plenty of fun to go around."

I didn't know what to say. I looked at Cami, who was staring back at me, her eyes wide. "Um, I'm not sure if her parents will let her," I said. This was a total lie, of course. Cami could announce to her parents that she wanted to spend the summer at the South Pole and they would say okay.

"Well, tell her to ask them and let me know," said my father. "Tell them not to worry, that Janie and I will be watching out for both of you. Just call me back soon and let me know so I can make a second reservation."

I hung up the phone and turned to Cami.

"Don't tell me," she said. "I've just won an exciting all-expenses-paid dream vacation to Beaverkill."

I shrugged and laughed. "If you want. My dad said I could bring you."

Cami thought a minute. Then she grinned. "Well, it's got to beat hanging around here without you, Jess."

"Are you sure you don't mind missing the cruise?" I asked her.

She waved a hand dismissively. "Are you kidding? I told you, I've already been to the Bahamas three times. I was only going because of you. But

23

what about you? The love of your life is going to be on that cruise."

"I know," I said glumly. "But it doesn't look like I can get out of this." I smiled. "And at least if I'm going to do time in jail, you'll be my cellmate."

Cami raised her eyebrows. "Anyway, who knows? Maybe you'll find a new love of your life up in the mountains."

"Oh, yeah, sure," I said. "I'm going to meet Mr. Wonderful and dance the night away at the Golden's Resort disco."

Cami looked interested. "They have a disco?"

"Don't get your hopes up, Cami," I advised. "Remember, my *dad* picked this place. It's probably full of old people."

Cami shrugged. "So? Nothing wrong with an older guy. Somebody experienced, sophisticated. Mmmm, I'm starting to like this idea. Does Mr. Wonderful have a friend for me?"

I laughed. Leave it to Cami to see the bright side—or should I say the *guy* side—of any situation. And knowing Cami, she probably *would* find somebody up in the Catskills. But not me. I wasn't even planning on looking.

I was totally hooked on Jeremy and determined to get together with him no matter what, even if it meant waiting until September.

I was just going to have to get used to the idea that this *wasn't* going to be my summer of first love after all.

# FOUR

I'LL NEVER FORGET the expression on Janie's face as she and my father watched Cami and me come down the walkway from the plane. Janie started out with this big, fake smile, but as we got closer you could see this wave of something come over her—dread, maybe, or even panic. Her eyes opened really wide, and her mouth kind of collapsed, revealing her huge white teeth.

"Hi, Jess! Hi, honey!" my dad yelled, waving his arms. He seemed completely oblivious to the fact that the person standing right next to him was entering a state of shock.

I guess Janie's reaction probably had something to do with Cami. Cami's hair was in about a hundred tiny braids, each one fastened with a different little kids' plastic barrette at the bottom. She was wearing this combat green jumpsuit with pink sequin-covered high-top sneakers, and dark purple lipstick with matching nail polish. Amazingly, she looked great. Like I said, Cami looks great in anything.

We got to the end of the walkway, and my dad gave me a big bear hug. It felt weird to hug him—familiar and strange at the same time. I hadn't seen him in almost two months, since the last time he was passing through Miami.

My dad and I stepped apart, and the four of us looked at each other for a moment. Janie managed to rearrange her face into something like a smile. Correction: She got the bottom part of her face to smile, but her eyes still looked like she was tied to a train track with a locomotive headed straight for her.

Cami was the first one to speak. "Hi," she said, sticking out her hand toward my father. "I'm Cami. Thanks very much for inviting me up here, Mr. Graham."

One thing about Cami—she can really turn on the charm when she wants to.

My father paused a moment. I think he was a little taken aback by Cami's appearance too. Then he smiled and shook Cami's hand. "My pleasure. Great to have you, Cami."

Cami turned to Janie, who was looking at her as if she were afraid she might catch whatever it was Cami had. "And you must be Janie Baxter. It's so incredibly great to meet you."

"It is?" said Janie. She cleared her throat. "Excuse me, I mean, nice to meet you too, Cami. And Jess, dear, so wonderful to see you again."

She leaned forward a little, almost as if she expected me to hug her. But I stayed where I was.

Janie looked flustered. She cleared her throat again. "How was the flight, girls?"

I shrugged. "Okay."

"I love airplanes," Cami said enthusiastically. "Those little soaps are the best, don't you think?"

"Um, yes, well, I suppose they're very convenient," Janie replied.

I stifled another laugh. Watching Janie and Cami together for four whole weeks was definitely going to be entertaining. They even *looked* funny together—Cami with her braids and dark lipstick next to Janie in her neat white slacks and perky pink polo shirt. Janie's blond hair was almost the exact color of Cami's, although Janie's was arranged into this helmet-shaped thing that must have been held in place by a ton of spray. Still, to a stranger, they probably looked like they could be mother and daughter—a mother and daughter with a generation gap the size of the Grand Canyon, that is.

"Peter," Janie said, "we'd better get going. I'm sure there can't be anyplace acceptable to stop for dinner anywhere near here."

*Not if you're the type of person who sends her food back to the chef over and over again,* I wanted to add. But I kept quiet.

"Besides," Janie went on, "I want to beat the crowd. You know I can't stand sitting in rush hour traffic."

27

"Janie's right," said my father. "Let's go get that luggage of yours, girls."

I glanced at Cami. She turned away from Janie and crossed her eyes and stuck out her tongue a little. I stifled a laugh. It sure was going to make things easier having Cami along on this trip.

Later that evening my father pulled up the car in front of a giant stucco building with wood trim surrounded by trees.

"Well, here we are!" he boomed happily.

I peered out of the window into the darkness.

"What's it like?" asked Cami, who was sitting next to me in the backseat.

"I can't see much," I answered. "Just a lot of trees and this big building."

My father was already halfway out of the car. "Come on, girls; come on, Janie. Let's go check in."

Janie was in the front seat, using a compact mirror to meticulously reapply her pale pink lipstick. Cami looked at me and did a perfect imitation of the way Janie was pursing her lips and raising her eyebrows.

Cami and I climbed out of the car, and my father handed the keys to an attendant in a green jacket. The night mountain air was really cool, and I shivered in my thin dress. Cami stretched her arms and cracked all ten of her knuckles, one at a time. Janie, who had just gotten out of the car, looked away. Already I could see that Janie wished my father hadn't said I could bring a friend. I didn't care. In fact, it made me happy that Janie didn't approve of Cami. After all, there were a few things Janie had done that I wasn't exactly thrilled about either. Like snatching my dad from us, for instance.

We all followed my father through a set of glass doors with the word *Golden's* painted on them in metallic gold script. Inside the building was a large lobby and lounge. Several clerks stood behind a long, polished wood counter, and a few hotel guests sat on the overstuffed leather furniture. Most of the people there looked about my father's age, although there was one family with twin girls who were probably about eleven.

"Make sure they give us a private bungalow, Peter. One with two rooms," Janie instructed as she and my father headed toward the check-in desk.

I flopped down on a huge leather couch in the lobby and sighed. Cami sat down beside me.

"I can't believe her," I whispered to Cami.

Cami grinned. "You mean Queen Janie?"

I nodded. That summed Janie up exactly. Janie was definitely the kind of person who thought she had to have things just so. And I could see already that she thought my father was the main person who was supposed to make it happen for her. Queen Janie and her trusty servant—my dad.

I leaned back against the couch. Cami's head was swiveling from left to right and back. I knew exactly what she was looking for.

"Forget it, Cami," I whispered, laughing a

29

little. "There's nobody interesting here, believe me." I sighed, thinking of Jeremy. "And you'd better get used to it because it's going to be like this all summer."

Cami raised her eyebrows. "Is it really? I'm glad to hear that." She nodded back toward the check-in desk.

There, standing a few yards away from my father and Janie, were two men. One of them was short and stocky, with a nearly bald head and a white handlebar mustache. He looked about fifty. The other guy was a lot younger, maybe even close to our age. He was tall and well built, with short, thick dark hair and very fair skin. He was wearing a dark blue warm-up suit.

The two men were talking to each other. I strained to listen, and it was a few moments before I realized that they weren't speaking English.

"Cute, huh?" asked Cami.

"I don't even think he's American," I told her.

"I know, isn't that kind of thrilling?" she responded. She turned to me. "Jess, I'm on a mission this summer. I want to go out with somebody really *different* while I'm here."

"Well, not speaking a word of English would be different," I remarked. I watched the two men, who seemed to be having a problem communicating with the desk clerk.

"It wouldn't matter," Cami assured me. She batted her eyelashes dramatically. "Just as long as he speaks the language of *love*." She laughed.

My father and Janie approached us. Behind them was a bellman in a forest green-and-gold uniform, pushing a huge cart with our suitcases on it. Correction: The cart was actually probably a normal size, but it looked huge because the bellman who was pushing it was tiny. He also seemed to be about a million years old.

"Okay, gang, here we go," said my father cheerfully. "Our rooms are in the Galaxy Circle."

"Watch out for that small blue suitcase," Janie instructed the bellman. "There are fragile items inside. Oh, and Peter, I think you'd better carry my briefcase. It's full of important papers."

My dad picked up the briefcase, and we followed him and Janie through the lobby, with the bellman right behind us.

"Galaxy Circle, what does that mean?" Cami asked in a low voice.

I shrugged. "Beats me," I whispered. "All I know is I'd like to send Janie off to another galaxy—for good."

It turned out that Galaxy Circle was a circular group of bungalows that were separate from the main hotel building. Each of the bungalows was named after a planet. You reached the circle by following a little illuminated, tree-lined path behind the main building, which was kind of nice. It was only about a five-minute walk, but by the end I was convinced that the bellman was going to have a heart attack. He was breathing heavily, and the little wisps of white hair on top of his head

31

were plastered down with sweat. I hoped my dad planned on giving him a good tip.

Our bungalow was Mercury. I have no idea why; there didn't really seem to be anything Mercury-ish about it—just a sign that said so. I guess it was supposed to sound impressive or something. My dad and Janie had the front room, and Cami and I had an adjoining one in the back. Each room had its own direct entrance off the path. The little old bellman dropped my dad and Janie off in their room first and then brought Cami and me back to ours.

Our room had two double beds with green-and-white-flowered bedspreads and green carpeting, a green night table, and a large green dresser. At the far end of the room was a white wicker table with a glass top and two matching chairs. One of those dopey hotel paintings of a lake scene hung on the wall above it.

We watched as the bellman struggled to unload our suitcases into the room.

"Do you think we should help him?" Cami whispered.

I shrugged. "He might get offended. I mean, it's his job, right? But it might be a good way to try to get to know him a little better," I said under my breath.

Cami looked at me like I was crazy. "What are you talking about?"

I snickered. "Well, you said you were looking for an older guy," I reminded her. "Somebody really different."

Cami swatted me. "Very funny, Jess." She looked back appraisingly at the bellman, who was putting the last of our suitcases down. "I do kind of like his outfit, though—although *I'd* never wear the pants and the jacket together like that."

When the bellman had left, I started to unpack, and Cami sat down at the wicker table and began leafing through some brochures.

"Nice pool," she commented, glancing at a glossy photo. "I wonder if Mr. Warm-up Suit from the lobby likes to swim."

"He looked sort of like the weight-lifting type to me," I said as I threw some T-shirts into a dresser drawer. "Do they have a gym?"

"Yeah, actually, they do," said Cami, glancing through some more pamphlets. "And horseback riding and tennis too. You know, this place might be kind of fun, Jess. Oh, and look, here's the calendar of special events. Hey, it says there's going to be a big barbecue and outdoor dance on the Fourth of July, with fireworks and stuff."

At the mention of the Fourth of July, I felt a pang. I couldn't help thinking of Jeremy and the Bahamas. I wondered what Jeremy was doing right then. Could he be thinking about me too? And what would he think when I didn't show up on the cruise?

I glanced up and saw Cami looking at me.

"Hey, Jess, you'll see him in the fall," she reminded.

I smiled. Cami always knew what I was thinking.

33

"Yeah, I know," I answered. Then I laughed. "I just can't believe I spent all that money on that white bikini and now he's not even going to see it!"

"You could always wear it to school the first day in September," Cami suggested.

"Oh, nice idea," I replied, rolling my eyes.

"Well, you have to admit, it would probably get Jeremy's attention," said Cami.

We both burst out laughing.

Just then there was a knock on the door that connected our room to my dad and Janie's.

"Come in!" I called.

My dad stuck his head in. "You girls all settled in here? Everything okay with the room?"

"Yeah, everything's fine, Dad," I answered.

"Just great, Mr. G.," added Cami.

"Super." My father looked pleased. "Well, make sure you get to sleep soon," he advised. "We've got loads of great activities to tackle tomorrow, and breakfast is at eight."

"Eight o'clock?" Cami's eyes looked like they were about to pop out of her head.

I was pretty surprised too. "Dad, isn't that kind of early? I mean, isn't this supposed to be vacation?"

My father laughed. "Jess, honey, when I was your age, I spent all my vacations on my grandparents' farm in Nebraska. I'd be up every morning at five to help with the chores, the milking and the chickens and everything. By eight o'clock I was practically ready for *lunch*. Besides, you don't want to miss what they have to offer for breakfast around here. Well, good night, girls. See you in the morning."

He closed the door, and Cami turned to me. "Jess, I'm sorry to have to be the one to break this to you, but I think your father might be crazy. *Lunch?*"

I laughed. "He's always talking about that farm stuff. Sometimes I wonder why he didn't just go to Nebraska and become a farmer, why he ever wanted to be a lawyer in the first place."

Cami shrugged. "I guess the money's better." She shook her head. "Eight o'clock, wow. This better be *some* breakfast."

"Yeah," I said, laughing.

What I didn't know then was that my first breakfast at Golden's was going to be one of the most important meals of my whole life.

# FIVE

THE FOLLOWING MORNING Cami and I followed my father and Janie down the path toward the main building.

As we walked I heard a telephone ring. Janie paused and took a cellular phone out of her shoulder bag. "Hello? Oh, hi, Kevin. How's that research going? I see. Listen, let me call you back, okay?" She closed the phone and slipped it back in her bag.

My father looked at her. "Everything okay?"

She nodded. "I've got that new paralegal helping me out on the Hunter girls' case. He's run into a little snag. Nothing serious, I'm sure. Come on, let's go to breakfast."

We entered the main building and walked into the dining room, a large sunny room with plate glass windows overlooking the mountains.

A hostess approached us. "Four in your party?"

"Yes, that's right," my father answered.

36

"Right this way, please."

As we followed the hostess across the crowded room a few people turned to stare at us. I knew it was probably because of Cami's outfit. The funny thing was, she didn't even look that wild, at least for Cami. She had on a gathered red miniskirt with cowboy boots printed all over it, a red-and-black-striped baby tee, and red heart-shaped sunglasses. But the crowd there was pretty conservative. Most of the people in the dining room were dressed like Janie—in pastel sports clothes. I supposed that even *I* looked a little out of place in my purple-and-white polka-dot sundress.

The hostess showed us to a large table where two couples who looked about my grandparents' age were sitting. The hostess indicated the four empty seats at the table. "Your server will be with you shortly."

I stared at the table in surprise. Were we really supposed to sit with these people? We didn't even know them!

"Hello, there!" bellowed one of the men at the table. He had one of those funny old-guy hairdos where they grow one piece really long and comb it over the top of their heads, hoping nobody will notice that they're basically bald. He grinned. "Have a seat. Park it right there, folks. Plenty of room for everyone. I'm Herb Relleck. The little lady here is Cora. But we've got no idea who these two characters across the table are; they just followed us up here. We think they're, whaddayacallit—*stalkers*."

He burst out laughing. "Just kidding. This is Mick and Frannie Carmichael, our best buddies."

I turned to my father. Obviously this man was crazy, and we should get out of there as soon as possible and find another table.

But to my surprise, my father pulled out the chair next to the man. "Hello, Herb," he said cheerfully. "I'm Peter Graham. This is my fiancée, Janie; my daughter, Jess; and her friend Cami."

"Very nice to meet you all," said Janie, taking the seat next to my father. "Go on and sit down, girls."

So Dad was *already* introducing Janie as "my fiancée." I glanced at Cami. She shrugged and pulled out the empty chair beside Mick Carmichael, who was wearing a white T-shirt that said Don't Ask Me—I'm on Vacation! and that barely covered his huge stomach.

I slid into my place beside Cami as my dad and Janie started talking to the others.

"I can't believe we got up at eight o'clock for this," I whispered.

"I think they're kind of cute," Cami replied. "And I love this guy's T-shirt," she added in a low voice. "Wouldn't it be great to wear that to school?"

I laughed. "Yeah, but on you it would probably be a dress."

A red-haired waiter in a white shirt and green pants came over to our table and put down a huge pitcher of orange juice.

"Good morning, everyone," he said in a chipper voice. "We have several things I'd like to tell you about today, including our famous four-egg omelettes: Today's special omelettes are a three-cheese omelette with spinach and mushrooms, and a sausage, onion, and tomato omelette. Those come with a large side of our special crinkle-cut potatoes and your choice of toast, an English muffin, or a bagel. We're also serving your choice of blueberry or banana pancakes and jumbo Belgian waffles with maple syrup, whipped cream, and strawberries."

Just listening made me feel full. "I think I'll just have an English muffin," I said.

"Oh, come on, now!" bellowed Mr. Relleck. "You're not having one of the specials? You gotta have one of the specials!" He turned to the waiter. "Bring her a plate of those waffles."

"No, really," I objected. "I'm not that hun—"

"But you gotta have one of the specials!" Mr. Relleck yelled again. "Go on. It's on me!"

Somehow I had the idea that it wasn't going to be too easy to win this one. "Okay, sure, bring me the waffles," I said.

"I'll have the waffles too," said Cami with a shrug.

"There you go!" Mr. Relleck said, obviously pleased.

The waiter left, and Cora Relleck began pouring orange juice into glasses. She was incredibly tan and had hair that had been dyed bright red. "So, girls," she said, peering across the table, "Jennie and

Carrie, is it? How are you enjoying your stay here?"

I cleared my throat. "Actually it's *Jess* and *Cami*," I corrected her. "And we just got here last—"

"What was that?" she cut me off. "Jerri and Connie?"

"Um, no," I said, trying not to laugh. "*Jess* and *Cami*. It's not important, really—"

"Well, of *course* it's important!" Mrs. Relleck said sharply. "They're your names, aren't they? Now tell me again, and for goodness' sake, *enunciate*."

"*Jessss* and *Cam-eee*," I said as slowly and loudly as I could. I glanced at my father, who was deep in conversation with Herb. It was bad enough that I was stuck talking to this woman who couldn't even hear me. Now she was actually getting *mad* at me!

"Actually it's *Chevy* and *Camry*, like the cars," Cami said.

The woman's face brightened. "All right, then! Why didn't you say so? We drive a Chevy, you know. Cavalier." She paused and wrinkled her forehead. "Chevy and Camry, is it? Isn't that a bit unusual?"

"Oh, no," Cami assured her. "Tons of people are naming their kids after cars these days. Our school's full of kids like us. Let's see, there's Lexus, and Mustang, and Jetta. And of course the twins, Civic and Accord. Oh, and then there's Jimmy. But that's a little different because he was named after a

40

car that was named after a *name*, if you know what I mean."

By this point I was laughing incredibly hard. Correction: I was trying incredibly hard *not* to laugh but not very successfully. Mrs. Relleck had this completely bewildered look on her face—she was sort of frozen like that, holding on to the orange juice pitcher and leaning forward with her eyebrows raised—and Cami was casually sipping her orange juice. I sat there with my hand over my mouth, shaking and trying to get hold of myself before I did something completely dorky like spitting or snorting. I kicked Cami under the table.

*Major* correction: I *tried* to kick Cami under the table. I *thought* I was kicking Cami under the table. What I actually turned out to be doing was kicking the leg of the table—hard. And unfortunately I did this just as Cami was putting her glass of orange juice down.

The glass tipped over instantly, spilling juice everywhere.

"Oh, no!" I cried, reaching for the glass. But there was already a huge puddle on the white table-cloth, and it was spreading.

Everyone stopped talking and stared for a moment.

"Here, take this!" Janie passed me her napkin.

"Don't worry, doll, we'll get the boy over to clean it up," said Mr. Relleck. He began to look around and snap his fingers. "Hello? Hello? We need some help over here!"

41

"What happened? What happened?" Mrs. Relleck was screaming.

I wished everyone would stop making such a big deal about it. I felt like every person in the room was staring at me.

Finally a waiter from another table arrived and started mopping at the puddle on the tablecloth in front of me with a rag. I didn't look up at first, didn't see his face, so to me he was just a green T-shirt and a pair of jeans with a rag in his hand. Then as he continued wiping I saw that some of the liquid was headed straight for the edge of the table—and my lap!

"Aaah! Watch out!" I cried. I jumped up out of my seat, bumping into him a bit.

"Sorry about that," he said in a low voice.

I turned to face him for the first time—and looked straight into a pair of the biggest, deepest brown eyes I'd ever seen. I caught my breath. With those dark eyes, strong cheekbones, and slightly curling lips, the face in front of me was handsome, but more than that too. It was as if those eyes, looking directly at me through those thick, dark lashes, could actually *speak* to me—as if they were communicating directly with something deep inside me.

Suddenly I couldn't move. Couldn't speak, couldn't do anything. The rest of the world had disappeared. The restaurant and everybody in it had faded into the background, and the two of us were frozen in place.

We stood there like that for a moment, staring into each other's eyes, before he shifted his gaze downward.

"Um, your dress," he said. His voice was husky, a little bit hoarse. It made my insides go all soft.

I looked down and saw that the front of my sundress had a huge wet spot on it. I didn't care. I smiled. "Oh, right."

"Here." He dabbed quickly at the area of my stomach with his rag, then stopped awkwardly. "Sorry," he mumbled, shaking a piece of his longish, dark brown hair out of his eyes. He turned his head away, but I could see the corners of his lips curl up into a smile.

I felt like I was about to melt into the floor.

"Jessie, dear, why don't you go back to the bungalow and put on something fresh?" suggested Janie.

I ignored her. Maybe if I stood here long enough, this guy would touch me again—even if it was with his rag.

Just then our waiter came hurrying over. "Oh, my, what happened here? Don't you worry about a thing. We'll get you cleaned right up." He turned to the gorgeous guy. "Danny, go tell Maurice to bring over a fresh tablecloth and reset these nice people so I can serve them their breakfast."

Danny.

*Danny.*

I held on to that name as I watched him walk away. There was something about him—something about his tall, slim frame and the way he swayed slightly as he walked, as if he were listening to music that no one else could hear, that made it impossible for me to take my eyes off him. I watched until he vanished somewhere on the far side of the room, and then I sank slowly back into my seat.

"Jessie, honey, are you sure you don't want to go change?" my father asked with concern.

"No, I'm all right," I answered, still in a daze.

"You ought to get them to reimburse you for the cleaning bill!" said Mr. Carmichael indignantly.

"Well, the hotel's not legally responsible, after all," Janie pointed out. "*They* didn't spill it on her."

"How *did* it happen, exactly?" Mrs. Carmichael asked.

"A shaky table leg, that's what it was, I'll bet!" answered Mr. Carmichael.

"Well, if that's the case, then the hotel would be liable for any damage, of course," agreed Janie.

I ignored them all. I still felt like everything around me was a dream—like the only thing that was real was those deep brown eyes, and the way they had locked onto mine. It had sent a warm feeling through me that made me want it to go on forever. Danny.

"It's all right. No harm done," my father said. "We'll get the dress cleaned. But Jess, are you sure you're okay like that? You're not cold?"

I shook my head.

"Don't worry about Jess," Cami advised knowingly. "I don't think she's cold at all. In fact, I'd say just the opposite." She lowered her voice and leaned toward me. "Feeling warm all over?"

I turned to look at her. Like I said, Cami always knows what I'm thinking. I felt myself start to smile. She grinned back at me.

Still, I was confused. What had just happened here? Had I really had a romantic moment with the *waiter,* of all people?

All I knew was that when I'd looked into those eyes, I'd experienced something brand-new. Something wonderful and warm. It wasn't anything like the way I'd felt when I was around Jeremy. Jeremy made me nervous, made me afraid I was going to trip over my own feet. Looking at this boy was almost the opposite—a sweet, melting, *safe* feeling.

And now, because of it, I was almost positive I'd never be the same again.

# SIX

"**G**O FOR IT, Jess!" Cami said for what seemed like about the hundredth time since breakfast.

"Cami, he *works* here," I argued. "Besides, I don't even know him."

"So what?" Cami countered. "That makes it more exciting." She raised her chin dramatically. "Just think—a mysterious stranger!"

We were changing into our bathing suits in a cabana by the pool. My dad and Janie had gone to play golf. They had invited us to go along, but somehow a game of golf didn't really sound that appealing. Besides, after that huge breakfast, Cami and I had agreed that we were too full and tired to even *think* about any activity that required more energy than lying in a lounge chair and applying suntan lotion.

"Cami, *you're* the one who wanted to meet someone different, not me," I reminded her.

"Besides," I added, slipping into my white bikini, "I like Jeremy, remember?" But even as I said it, I realized I sounded a little unsure. The truth was, I'd kind of forgotten about Jeremy until just that moment.

"Jess, admit it. You don't even really know Jeremy *either*," Cami pointed out. She adjusted a string on her bright orange suit. "He's just some guy you've been gawking at in English class all year."

"Well, at least I know who he *is!*" I responded. "I know his last name. I know who his friends are. I know how old he is. I know that he lives in South Beach like we do and that he goes to our school." For some reason I was getting upset. "I don't know *anything* about this Danny guy—only that he works at the hotel and that he probably lives somewhere around here." I paused before pushing open the cabaña door. "Cami, we're talking about my first love—something that I'll only experience once in my whole life. Somehow I just can't believe it's supposed to be with a waiter from Beaverkill!"

Cami shrugged. "Fine, have it your way." She pushed her sunglasses down onto her nose and followed me outside.

As usual, Cami's appearance created a sensation immediately. We had both agreed to wear our new bathing suits the first day, and Cami's bright orange thong was way skimpier than anything anyone else was wearing. Not to mention that she was the only girl there with a belly-button ring. On top of all that there was the fact that she's incredibly gorgeous and has the kind of body that's not supposed to exist in real life.

As we passed the poolside bar and headed toward the lounge chairs I kept my eyes front and tried to ignore the outright stares and tune out the whispers of everyone around us.

One thing I had to laugh at, though, was this kid who was trimming the hedges. He was wearing green Golden's coveralls, so I guess he worked there, but he looked kind of young, and he had a round face and a bunch of freckles. I guess when he caught sight of Cami, he just kind of froze in place, staring at her instead of looking at the bushes. The trouble was, the electric hedge clippers were still turned on. Without realizing what he was doing, the poor guy had already clipped that one hedge a lot shorter than the others. And it looked like if he didn't snap out of it soon, he was going to cut it down to nothing more than a little stump.

Of course, Cami was loving every minute of it. She blew him a kiss before she sat down on her lounge chair, and he nearly dropped his clippers into a giant rosebush. She giggled. "This place is fun."

"I guess," I answered. I wasn't sure why, but I was feeling kind of down suddenly.

Cami turned to me. "Listen, Jess, you've got it bad for this guy, I can tell. You've got all the symptoms."

I lay back in my lounge chair. "I do?"

"I saw the way you were looking at him at breakfast," she answered, starting to apply some suntan lotion to her legs. "And the way he was looking at you too."

I sat up. "He was looking at me?" I repeated. So it hadn't been my imagination. Cami had seen it too. "How?"

"Oh, pretty much the same way he is right now," Cami responded in a casual tone.

*"What?"* Now I wanted to kill her. "What are you talking about?" I whispered urgently. "He's here? Where?"

Cami nodded nonchalantly across the pool to the left. I turned my head and was shocked to see Danny standing beside an empty lounge chair with a stack of towels under one arm. As soon as he saw me looking at him he shifted his gaze. A moment later he loped off toward the cabanas.

"Pretty versatile, huh?" commented Cami. "He waits tables, delivers towels. . . . I wonder if he'll be putting on a floor show later."

"Oh, my gosh," I breathed. Suddenly I longed to gaze into Danny's eyes again. But I was confused too. I was supposed to be head over heels for Jeremy, wasn't I? "What am I going to do?" I groaned.

"I still say go for it," Cami replied. "Hey, listen, put some of this stuff on my back, okay?" She handed me a tube of suntan lotion and twisted around in her chair.

I sat up and started rubbing the lotion on her back. "Go for it—easy for you to say."

Cami lifted her hair and bent forward. When she spoke again, her voice was slightly muffled. "Look, Jess, this shouldn't be too hard. You're both stuck up here for four weeks together, right? And so far it looks like it's not going to be too tough to find him, since he seems to have about a million jobs around this place. Just talk to him."

I squeezed some more lotion into the palm of my hand. "Talk to him," I repeated. "How? About what?"

"About anything. It doesn't matter," Cami said from under her mop of ringlets. "Start up a conversation at breakfast. Spill some more juice on yourself. Whatever—"

Suddenly I spotted Danny coming out of the cabana area with more towels. He started toward us.

"Cami," I said softly. "He's coming."

But she didn't hear me. "Talk about waiter stuff. Or towels."

Danny was getting closer. He'd be right by our chairs in a moment.

*"Cami,"* I whispered urgently. "Quiet."

"Towels, that's it," Cami continued, oblivious. "After all, you're a guest, he's a towel guy, right? Towels are something you have in common. Just walk up to him and ask him if you can have a—"

Danny was right in front of us. I pinched Cami's back as hard as I could to shut her up.

"Ouch!" she yelled indignantly. She flipped her hair back. "What did you do that for?" She glanced up and saw Danny standing above her. "Oops. I mean, hi. Oh, towels, great!" She turned to me and grinned. "We were just talking about towels, right?"

I stared up at Danny, barely able to answer. "Towels, that's right," I replied softly.

Danny gave me one of those little half smiles, like when he'd tried to wipe the orange juice off my dress. I smiled back. Suddenly everything I'd said in the cabana—about Jeremy, about first love and

50

what it was supposed to be—none of it mattered at all. Suddenly the only thing I wanted was to look into Danny's deep brown eyes forever. Correction: I wanted more than that. I wanted to feel his strong arms close around me, pulling me to him. I longed to experience his lips touching mine.

I wondered what it would feel like to kiss him.

"Want one?" he asked in his slightly husky voice.

I was startled. *What?* Had he just read my mind or something? Then I realized what he meant. "Oh, a towel. Sure." I stood up.

Cami looked briefly at her wrist. "Oh, gee, look at that. Time for my morning swim." She stood up.

I tried not to smile. Cami was being pretty obvious. I wondered if Danny had noticed that she wasn't even wearing a watch.

"Well, catch you two later." Cami took a couple of steps to the edge of the pool and dove in, creating a huge splash.

Danny and I both jumped back from the spray.

"Looks like today's my day to get soaked," I commented.

He grinned. "Yeah." He handed me a towel. "Guess you could have used this at breakfast."

"Right." I laughed.

"Is your dress okay?" he asked.

"Oh, yeah, fine," I answered. "I mean, I'll just wash it."

"Good," he said. He shook a lock of hair from his eyes. "It's a pretty dress."

"Thanks." We both stood there a little awkwardly.

"So," I said finally. "What's it like working here?"

He glanced down at his sneakers and shrugged one shoulder. "Okay, I guess. You get to do the activities when you have time off."

"That sounds nice," I said. "We just got here yesterday, so there's a bunch of things I haven't even seen yet."

"Yeah, there's a lot of stuff to do. Boating. Tennis. Tonight's movie night," he informed me. "Every Thursday. Sometimes I go."

"Oh." I wasn't sure what to say. Why was it starting to seem like every guy I liked was always *talking* about the movies around me but never actually asking me to go with them?

"It's some old movie," he continued. "*Back Window* or something."

"You mean *Rear Window*?" I said with excitement. "That's a great movie!"

He looked down at his sneakers. "Sounds like you've already seen it."

"Only about seven times. It's one of my absolute favorites. I love Hitchcock," I explained.

He shrugged one shoulder. "Well, maybe I'll see you there. You know, if you decide to go."

"Yeah, okay, sure," I said. I felt funny. Was this supposed to be like a date?

"I better get back to work," he told me. "Catch you later." He turned to go and then paused. "Hey, what's your name anyway?"

"Jessica," I answered. "Jessica Graham."

He nodded. "Danny Jordan. See you, Jessica."

"Okay, bye." I watched him walk away.

After he was gone, I stood there for a minute, not sure what to do. My heart felt like it was beating a mile a minute, and I couldn't get the smile off my face. I looked around for Cami.

I spotted her at the far end of the pool, dripping wet and perched on a stool at the bar. Sitting beside her was the guy we'd seen in the lobby the night before, the one she called Mr. Warm-up Suit. Today he was wearing gray sweatpants with a tight white T-shirt that showed his muscles.

Amazingly, he and Cami seemed to be having a conversation. I supposed I must have been wrong, that this guy must speak English after all. Whatever it was he was saying, Cami looked more than interested. She was leaning toward him and nodding enthusiastically.

I sat back down in my chair. I was dying to tell Cami about what had just happened with Danny, but I didn't want to interrupt whatever was going on. I closed my eyes and smiled to myself, thinking of how determined Cami had been to meet someone different this summer.

It looked like maybe she wasn't the only one it was going to happen to after all.

# SEVEN

"WHAT DO YOU think, Jess?" Cami stood in the center of our room in the Mercury bungalow, modeling her leopard-print cropped top, black microshorts, and black motorcycle boots.

"Pretty hot," I told her. "Where did you say this guy was from?"

"Bulgaria," she answered. "Or he was born in Yugoslavia, but now he lives in Bulgaria or something. Or maybe it's that he's from Bulgaria but he's been training in Yugoslavia. I'm not really sure."

I laughed. "I'm amazed you got *that* much straight, considering you don't even speak the same language."

"Believe me, it wasn't easy," said Cami. "I tried miming, and we drew pictures on cocktail napkins. That's how I found out he's a discus thrower—he drew à picture of this flying saucer thing." She laughed. "For about half an hour I just thought he was really into Frisbee." She peered at herself in the mirror above our dresser. "Mostly he just spoke his language and I spoke English and we smiled a lot. I just hope I got where and when I'm supposed to meet him right." She glanced at me. "Is that what you're wearing?"

I looked down at my blue-and-white-flowered top and faded jeans. "Yeah. I get the feeling Danny might be kind of the casual type. Besides," I added, "it's not like we made an actual, real date."

Cami shrugged. "In my book, as long as some-one says, 'You be there, I'll be there too,' it's a date. Anyway, you look nice."

"Thanks," I said.

"But you should take your hair down," she added.

I glanced at my reflection in the mirror. My hair was in a ponytail, fastened with a heart-shaped, mother-of-pearl barrette. Cami always says she likes my hair down, but I'm never sure. "You think?"

"No question," she replied. "It's much more ro-mantic looking. You've got great hair, Jess."

I shrugged and unfastened my barrette. Then I glanced at the clock on the night table. It was seven forty-five. "Oh, gosh," I said, my stomach doing a little flip-flop, "I better get going. The movie starts in fifteen minutes."

"I'll walk out with you," offered Cami. "I'm supposed to meet Lanz, or Franz, or whatever his name is, by the golf course."

I knocked quickly on the door that led to my fa-ther and Janie's room.

"Come in!" Janie called.

I opened the door. Janie, who was wearing glasses, was sitting at a table with papers and folders spread out in neat piles in front of her. I could hear the shower running in the bathroom. She looked up at me expectantly, peering over her glasses.

"I just wanted to let my dad know that I was going out for a while," I said. "There's a movie over in the main building."

"All right, dear," Janie said. "You girls enjoy yourselves."

Obviously she thought Cami was coming with me. I didn't bother to correct her. Somehow I thought it might be better not to explain to Janie about Lanz/Franz.

"What's playing?" Janie asked.

*"Rear Window,"* I told her.

"Oh, really?" she said. "Too bad we've made plans to meet another couple for drinks. Your father loves Hitchcock, you know."

"Yes, as a matter of fact, I do know," I answered, annoyed. "He and I used to rent Hitchcock films all the time. Back when he lived at *home*," I couldn't help adding.

Janie turned back to the papers on her desk. "I'll give him the message," she said curtly.

I turned and closed the door behind me. I didn't quite slam it, but I closed it hard enough to make sure Janie would notice.

Cami looked at me curiously.

I shook my head. "I can't stand her."

"Oh, you mean Painie?" Cami asked.

I laughed. "Exactly."

"Yeah, I know what you mean." Cami hooked her arm through mine. "Come on, sweetie. Time to forget all about her and go meet your dream date."

When we got outside, the sun was just going down behind a mountain to the west, and the little lights that lined the wooded path were coming on. The trees and the other bungalows looked serene in the fading light. I thought of Danny and felt another little flutter in my stomach—nothing like the nervous terror that always seemed to turn me into a block of wood when Jeremy was around—but a gentle, jittery feeling of anticipation.

When we got to the turnoff for the golf course, Cami gave me a quick hug. "Have fun."

"You too," I answered. Then I thought of something. "Hey, are you sure the golf course is open at night?"

She looked at me. "No, Jess, as a matter of fact, I'm almost positive it's *not* open." She raised her eyebrows. "That's the whole point."

I laughed. "Okay, I get it." I should have realized that Cami hadn't been planning on playing golf. "See you."

A few moments later the main building appeared through the trees. I felt a surge of excitement and skipped the last few steps to the back entrance.

The room where the movie was going to be shown was on the main floor, opposite the dining room. A few dozen rows of chairs had been set up, and I was kind of surprised to see how crowded it was.

I scanned the backs of the crowd, wondering what I should do. Was Danny there yet? Should I wait for him or sit right down? I was starting to doubt if there were even two available seats together.

Suddenly a voice interrupted my thoughts.

"Well, look who's here!"

I turned, expecting to see Danny. But it was Herb Relleck, with Cora Relleck standing beside him. They were dressed in matching green-and-white-checked shirts and white slacks.

"Oh, hi," I said, trying to hide my disappointment.

Mrs. Relleck peered at me. "Cavalier, wasn't it?"

"Excuse me?" I said.

"Cavalier," she repeated. "Or was it Chevy? That's it, I remember—Chevy and Camry!"

"Oh, yes," I said, realizing what she was referring to. "Yes, that's right." I glanced around quickly. "Well, I guess I'd better find a seat," I said, starting to move away.

Mr. Relleck put a hand on my arm to stop me. "Oh, you'll never find a seat, not now. It's all taken—reserved. You've got to be here early if you want a seat for the movie." He laughed maniacally. "You know what they say—early bird gets the worm, eh?"

I nodded. "I guess." *Get me out of here,* I thought.

"But never mind; you can sit with us," Mr. Relleck went on. "I saved four right over here, but it looks like Mick and Frannie aren't going to make it after all." He squeezed my arm. "Mick's got a bad case of the runs," he confided. "Something he ate at dinner."

Now I felt like I was about to throw up. And I was ready to panic too. It was bad enough that Danny didn't seem to be anywhere around, but now it looked like I was trapped here with the Rellecks. The last thing in the world I wanted was to watch the movie with them, especially if it meant hearing the disgusting details of Mr. Carmichael's digestive problems. It would probably ruin *Rear Window* for me forever.

Just then I spotted Danny waving to me from a spot near the center of the room. Beside him was an empty seat. I smiled and waved back.

"Thanks a lot anyway," I said to Mr. and Mrs. Relleck. "But someone already got me a seat. Maybe next time," I added, hurrying away.

I made my way to where Danny was sitting just as the lights were being lowered.

"Hi," I whispered.

"Hey," he whispered back.

"Thanks for saving me a seat," I said, sliding into my spot as the opening credits began.

He shook his hair out of his eyes. "Yeah, I figured I better."

"Shhh!" hissed a voice somewhere behind us. We smiled at each other and then both turned and focused on the screen.

It was weird, watching the movie beside Danny. It was pretty hard to concentrate, for one thing. Of course, I'd already seen *Rear Window* a bunch of times, so it wasn't like I had to pay very close attention. It was funny, though, spending all that time sitting right next to somebody I had just met and not even being able to talk to him.

I kept wondering if Danny was going to make some kind of move—put his arm around me or something. That's what I'd always imagined a guy was supposed to do in the movies. At least that's what they always seemed to do on TV. Of course, I'd never actually been to the movies with a guy before. Correction: I'd been to the movies with several guys, if you counted junior high school, when a bunch of kids all used to go to a movie together in a big crowd. But the closest thing I'd ever had to a guy making a move on me in a movie theater was back in seventh grade when Marcus McGurney accidentally tripped over my foot trying to get down the aisle and landed on my lap. Believe me, Marcus McGurney wasn't anybody you'd want making a move on you anyway.

Well, as it turned out, Danny didn't do anything more than that either. Basically he pretty much just sat there next to me. There were a couple of times when our arms brushed against each other's, which seemed sort of meaningful to me, but I couldn't really tell if he was noticing it the way I was.

I even considered faking being scared a couple of times so I could sort of hold on to him. If you've never seen it, *Rear Window* has some pretty scary parts; it's all about this guy who watches out the window of his apartment and discovers that there's been a grisly murder in another apartment across the courtyard. But since I'd already told Danny that I'd seen the movie a bunch of times, it seemed like it might be kind of a stretch to act like I was really scared by it. Anyway, I wasn't sure I could actually go through with faking something like that. It seemed like a pretty silly way to get close to someone.

Finally the last scene came to a close. As the film wound down with the final credits a few people applauded. The lights went back on.

Danny turned to me. "That was really good."

I nodded. "Like I said, it's one of my favorites."

We started to thread our way through the seats with the rest of the crowd. Suddenly I spotted Mr. Relleck, waving wildly at me.

"Oh, no," I moaned. The last thing I wanted was to get into another embarrassing conversation with him, especially with Danny at my side.

"What's going on?" Danny looked concerned.

I shook my head. "Oh, nothing. Just somebody I don't really want to see right now."

Danny followed my gaze. "Oh, you mean that guy in the checks? Isn't he your grandfather or something?"

I stared at him. "My grandfather? No way."

Danny looked away. "Sorry. It's just that you were sitting with him at breakfast, so I—"

"Oh, right," I said, realizing why he'd made the mistake. "No, those two old couples were just some people that the waitress put us with."

Danny laughed a little. "Yeah, that's that 'family style' thing. They love that around here."

"Yeah, well, I don't," I replied. "And I bet none of those people who love it ever had to eat breakfast with that group!" I groaned. "Oh, forget it, we're trapped. He's coming this way."

"Come on, I know another exit," Danny said quickly. "We'll go out the back." He grabbed my hand.

Danny pulled me back through the crowd toward the other end of the room. Of course, the fact that we were suddenly holding hands now wasn't exactly something that escaped me. In fact, I think I probably would have agreed to stay and talk to Mr. Relleck all night if Danny would keep holding my hand.

Danny pulled me around the back of the movie screen and opened a door. Before I knew it, we were outside.

I laughed. "That was great. Thanks."

Danny grinned. "No problem."

We started walking. We were still holding hands, which was perfectly fine with me. It was a little funny, though, the way both of us were sort of pretending not to notice—as if we'd just *forgotten* to let go of each other or something.

"I guess you know this place pretty well," I said.

"Yeah," said Danny. He paused and turned to me. "Want to see my favorite spot?"

"Okay," I answered.

This had to be, without a doubt, the most romantic moment of my life. Here I was, walking through the woods at night, holding hands with a boy who could make me feel like an ice-cream cake in July just by looking at me. I never wanted it to end.

Danny led me downhill along a path that went through a thickly wooded area. After a few minutes

I saw the sparkle of moonlight on water through the trees.

"The lake," Danny explained in a low voice. "Come on."

We followed the path along the shore of the lake, past some rowboats tied to a dock. The path dipped into the woods again and came out by a small clearing. In front of us was a porchlike building, open on all sides, with an octagonal floor and a roof supported by columns. Even at night I could see that the building was old and that it needed some repair. The paint on the columns was peeling, and the two small steps leading up to the platformlike floor were sagging.

Danny carefully led me up the steps. We walked across the floor together. The lake lay spread out in front of us, shimmering in the moonlight.

"This is incredible," I breathed. "What is this place?"

"The gazebo," Danny answered. "No one uses it anymore, but they used to have dances here in the old days."

"How amazing," I said a little wistfully, leaning lightly against a column. "How did you find out about it?"

"This guy Sam. He's one of the cooks. Sam's been here practically since the hotel was built," Danny explained.

"What about you?" I asked him. "How long have you been working here?"

"This is my first year," he answered. He looked away, at the lake. "And my last," he added in a low voice.

"Why?" I wondered out loud. "I mean, I thought you said it was an okay job."

"It is," he answered. "It's fine. It's just that I don't plan on being here next year."

"Oh." I wasn't sure what to say. "This is my first time here too," I told him. "Actually, I didn't even want to come at all, but my parents made me."

Danny looked at me and gave me one of his little half smiles. "I guess they knew what they were doing."

"Maybe so," I answered. I smiled back at him. "So far I don't miss home one bit."

He turned to me. "Where *is* home for you anyway, Jessica?"

"South Beach," I answered. "In Florida."

He gazed out at the lake. "Florida. That's pretty far away."

"I know," I answered softly.

I wondered if he was thinking what I was thinking, about the end of the summer. Even though I had just met him, the idea of going back home, of being over a thousand miles away from Danny, made me incredibly sad.

"Where do you live, Danny?" I asked him.

He shrugged a shoulder. "I've got a room here, in the staff building behind the tennis courts."

"No, I mean, where do you really live? You know, where are you from?"

He was silent a moment. "No place, really," he said at last.

I laughed a little. "Well, you have to be from somewhere," I told him.

He turned away and picked up a rock from the floor of the gazebo. "I've lived a bunch of places, that's all." He tossed the rock into the water.

We were silent for a few minutes. I watched him stare at the lake. *What's going on?* I wondered. *Is he angry about something? Things seemed to be going so well. Did I say something wrong?*

Danny kicked another stone into the water and turned to me. "Come on, I'll walk you back. What part of the hotel are you in?"

"Galaxy Circle," I answered in a low voice. I was disappointed. Disappointed and confused.

We walked silently back through the woods together. As I followed Danny up the path I felt a slow ache growing inside me. What was happening? Why had Danny decided to end our evening together so suddenly? Could it be that he didn't like me after all?

We followed the illuminated path that led to Galaxy Circle without a word. When we got to my bungalow, I stopped.

"This is it," I said without looking at him.

Danny looked at the sign on the outside of the little building.

"Mercury, huh?" He paused and took a deep breath. "You know, I used to kind of have a thing about Mercury when I was a little kid." His voice suddenly sounded far away. "Wherever we were, I'd always make sure I spotted it in the sky every night just after sunset." He laughed, his voice a little hoarse. "I used to say I was going to be the first as-tronaut on Mercury."

I smiled. "I used to be positive I was going to be an elephant trainer in the circus," I said, remember-ing. "Do you need a telescope to see Mercury?"

"No, not if you just want to spot it. It kind of looks like a big star," he answered. "I always wanted a telescope, though. My dad used to say he was going to get me one." He gave a little scornful laugh. "But he was always promising stuff like that, stuff he couldn't deliver."

I longed to ask him what he was talking about. The way he talked about his dad, I got the feeling he might not be around anymore. But something in Danny's voice told me that it wasn't easy for him, talking like this. I decided not to press him into telling anything more than he was ready to say.

"I guess I know what you mean," I said finally. "My dad made some promises too. Promises it turned out he wasn't going to keep." My voice cracked. It was weird, but suddenly I felt like I was about to cry. I turned away quickly and looked down at the roots of a tree near my sneaker.

Danny stepped closer to me. I continued to stare at the roots, hoping he wouldn't see the tears welling up in my eyes. *This is stupid,* I thought. *You haven't cried about Mom and Dad since the day they told you, over a year ago. Why are you suddenly getting all blubbery now?*

Danny softly cupped my chin in his hand. Gently he tilted my face up toward his.

66

There they were, right in front of me—those eyes. Those big, beautiful eyes. The eyes that had changed me forever over spilled orange juice that morning. As I looked into them now they seemed so serious, as if they were trying to tell me something very important. I blinked, and a tiny tear trickled down my cheek. Danny took his hand from my chin and carefully traced the tear's path with his finger. Then he put his hand at the base of my neck, in my hair. He moved his face closer to mine.

I closed my eyes. Ever so slowly, ever so softly, our lips met. The kiss was gentle and caring, and I felt a warmth spread slowly through my whole body. Danny put his other arm around me and I leaned into him, feeling as if I were falling through space. I was Alice in Wonderland, tumbling down a deep, dark tunnel to a whole new world. I was flying to the moon—to Mercury! I had lost all sense of direction, and I didn't care. I knew this was the moment I had waited for all my life.

When we pulled apart, Danny was gazing into my eyes. *I could stay here forever,* I thought. And Danny's eyes seemed to say the same thing.

That's when I heard Janie's voice coming toward me, loud and clear through the trees. "Oh, I knew I *never* should have worn these shoes up here! They're getting soil on them from the path. Peter, did you remember to reserve court time for us tomorrow?"

"Sure did. I got us a court at ten-thirty," my father answered.

I shrank back into the shadow of a tree, pulling Danny with me as my father and Janie passed by on the path. I knew they would enter the bungalow from the front, where their room was, so I waited quietly for a moment.

Not that I thought my dad had any major objections against guys or anything, but I wasn't too sure how he'd like it if he found me kissing somebody in the woods at night like that. Besides, what I had with Danny was still new. I wasn't ready to share it with my dad—and certainly not with Janie!

"What's going on?" asked Danny in a whisper. He glanced around. "Are you hiding from more old people?"

I stifled a laugh. "Kind of," I whispered. "It's my father. I guess I better go inside," I added reluctantly.

Danny looked at me, and his eyes seemed as unwilling to say good-bye as I felt.

I stretched up on tiptoe and gave him one more quick kiss. Then I forced myself to turn away.

"Good night," I whispered, heading for the door of the bungalow.

A deep, husky whisper floated back to me from the shadows of the bungalow.

"Good night, Jess."

# EIGHT

THE NEXT MORNING I rolled over sleepily and glanced at the clock on the night table. It said nine-twenty.

*Nine-twenty!* I sat bolt upright.

"Cami! Cami!" I called to the lump of blankets on the other bed. "Oh, my gosh! Wake up!"

Cami rolled over and squinted grouchily through her mop of hair. "What?" she said in a gravelly voice.

"Cami, I think we missed breakfast!" I said urgently.

Cami's eyes closed. "Good," she growled.

"No, Cami, you don't understand!" I said. "This was my chance. Danny was probably working!"

There was a knock on the door that led to my father and Janie's room. My father poked his head in.

"Good morning, sleepyheads," he said cheerfully. "I thought I heard you talking in here."

"Dad, why didn't you wake us for breakfast?" I asked.

"Well, I could tell you two weren't too crazy about the early rising yesterday," he replied. "Besides, I wanted to make sure you were well rested for today's match."

"Match?" Cami repeated.

"Tennis," my father answered. "Doubles. You girls against us. Best of three. I've got a court for ten-thirty."

I stretched. "I don't know if I feel like playing tennis, Dad," I said.

Not that I didn't like tennis. I had a bunch of lessons when I was little, and my dad and I used to play sometimes before he moved out. It was fun. We used to cream his friends the Leonards in doubles. But I wasn't exactly crazy about the idea of playing with Janie. Besides, what if Danny was at the pool again?

"You'll feel like it when you get out there," my dad responded. He held out a little paper bag. "Here. We brought you a doggie bag from breakfast. Some muffins. Eat up and get dressed." He put the bag on the table and walked out, closing the door behind him.

"Well, that sounds pretty settled to me," Cami remarked.

I rolled my eyes. "That's my dad. Once he gets an idea, it's almost impossible to talk him out of it."

Cami laughed. "I guess that's pretty much how you and I ended up skipping that cruise to the Bahamas and coming here instead." She stood up, walked over to the table, and picked up the bag.

I smiled. "Yeah, but I'm starting to think that probably wasn't such a bad idea after all."

Cami raised her eyebrows. "Mmmm, sounds good. So how'd it go last night anyway? Are you in love?"

I hesitated a moment. Was I in love with Danny? Could I be in love with Danny, even though I'd just met him? I felt the warm glow return to my body, remembering the feeling of his lips on mine, the way he had looked at me.

"Maybe so," I said softly.

Cami's eyes widened. "Wow, Jess. This sounds serious!"

I smiled. "I tried to wake you up to tell you all about it when I got back, but you were completely asleep. You wouldn't budge."

Cami dug around in the bag for a muffin. "Yeah, I was really tired. I guess there must have been something strong in that drink."

"You were drinking?" Now I was a little concerned. Cami sober was wild enough—Cami drunk was a nightmare.

I'd only seen her like that once, actually, at this big open house party at the beginning of the school year. After watching her swim naked in the pool and sing "The Star-Spangled Banner" at the top of her lungs on the neighbors' front lawn, I'd spent the

71

rest of the night in an upstairs bathroom holding her hair back for her while she threw up in the toilet. It wasn't a pretty sight.

Luckily Cami usually stayed away from alcohol. That was why I was so surprised to hear she had been drinking last night.

"What about Lanz, or Franz? Was he with you?" I asked her.

Cami shook her head. "Things didn't really work out between us. Actually his coach found out he was meeting me and decided to break it up." She laughed. "His name turned out to be *Hans,* actually. Anyway, his coach thought I would distract him from his training. That's what they came up here for, to relax and work out in the gym and stuff and rest up for some big match. But I met a new guy. His name's Kirk. He's the bartender at the cocktail lounge here."

"So that's where you got the drinks," I said.

"Drink," Cami corrected. "It was just one. And I only had it because he said he was going to make something special for me. I told him I was eighteen. You have to be twenty-one here to get into a bar, but he let me hang out anyway." She grinned. "He's twenty-four."

I shook my head. "Well, there's your older guy, Cam."

Cami shrugged. "Yeah, we'll see. He seems okay. He's really cute. Anyway, tell me about Danny."

I stood up and walked over to the table. Cami

handed me a blueberry muffin. "There's not really that much to tell," I said, sitting down. "We saw the movie and then we went for a walk down by the lake. There's this old gazebo there that nobody uses anymore."

Cami wiggled her eyebrows. "So? Did it get hot and heavy?"

I felt myself blushing a little. "Well, not then, but later, when we said good night." I laughed. Then I sighed happily. "It was great, Cami."

"Hey, I bet Kirk and Danny know each other," said Cami enthusiastically. "You know, since they both work here. Kirk grew up right in the next town. It's called Deer Falls or Deer Creek or something."

"I don't know where Danny's from," I told her. "Actually, it's kind of funny. I don't know very much about him at all."

Cami grinned and bit into a chocolate chip muffin. "Well, it sounds like you guys were a little too busy to talk anyway."

I smiled. But I had a funny feeling inside about the whole thing. On one hand, there was no doubt in my mind that Danny and I were meant to be together. I'd felt it from the moment I first looked into his eyes. And he seemed to sense it too. We'd definitely made a real connection last night.

But the truth was, in many ways Danny Jordan was still a complete stranger to me. Was it really possible to feel this way about someone you didn't even know?

★     ★     ★

Two hours later Cami and I stood facing Janie and my father across the tennis court. It was Janie's serve, and we were all waiting while she bounced the ball up and down on the ground about a million times.

I looked at Cami and rolled my eyes. Janie was driving me crazy. She had to be the most annoying tennis player in the universe. When we first got there, she complained about the court because she thought the net was too slack and there was this little puddle in the corner. She made my dad go into the clubhouse and argue with the manager to get us another court, even though it was obvious that there weren't any others available since people were already playing on all the other courts. I was ready to tell Cami we should get out of there and forget about the whole thing—which probably would have made Janie pretty happy, since I could tell she wasn't pleased about playing with Cami, who was dressed in a pair of minuscule neon green stretch shorts and a zebra-striped bra top with her sparkly pink sneakers and belly button ring. But then this guy who was giving a tennis lesson to a little girl on the next court finished up, so we moved over there.

Of course my dad acted like he was actually pleased that we had switched courts, like he agreed with Janie that the first court hadn't been good enough, but I knew better. I was sure that if she hadn't been there, he wouldn't even have noticed the net and the puddle on the first court. Or if he had, he definitely wouldn't have made a big deal out of it.

But Janie was the kind of person who had to make a big deal out of everything. She was very particular. Like now, with her serve.

She stopped bouncing the ball and wrinkled her forehead disapprovingly. "Peter, I don't like these balls. Are you sure these are from the fresh can we brought with us?"

"That's right," my father responded cheerfully.

Janie frowned. "Well, then, it's a bad can."

I turned my back to them and looked at Cami. I rolled my eyes again. She grinned at me.

"Here, try one of these," I heard my father say. I turned around as he tossed Janie a ball.

Janie looked at the neon orange ball with disgust. "It's *orange*."

My father grinned. "Yeah, I know. Cute, huh? I picked them up at the Sports Shop before we left New York."

"I prefer the regular yellow ones," Janie said curtly. She tossed the ball up in the air and served. Her serve was so sudden that it flew by me and I missed it.

"Oh, thanks a lot!" I said angrily.

"Got to keep on your toes, Jessie," my father said cheerfully. "That's forty-thirty, our advantage."

"Just let them win," Cami muttered. "They won the first set, and it's best of three, right? Let them have it, and we can get out of here."

I picked up the ball. "No way," I told her angrily.

I glared at Janie, standing there in her perky red-white-and-blue tennis dress and matching headband and wristbands, and I think I hated her more than ever at that moment. And I hated my dad for the way he did everything she wanted. At the first chance I slammed the ball out of the air over the net. It ripped down the center of the court and hit the ground. Janie dove for it and barely managed to return it. I felt satisfaction spread through me.

"Nice one, Jess!" my dad called as Cami returned Janie's shot.

My dad lobbed it back to me, and I smashed it back—right past Janie.

"Yes!" I shouted. I turned to Cami and we high-fived.

Janie had an annoyed look on her face.

"Forty-forty, deuce. We're tied," I reminded them.

My father took another orange tennis ball out of his pocket. "Okay, Janie, come on. Two more points for the game, and the set and the match are ours. Let's see that stuff."

I was stung. *Let's see that stuff*—that's what he always used to say to *me!* Then it struck me—in the past, whenever we played doubles, my dad and I had always been on the same side, against my dad's friends the Leonards.

Janie served. As the ball flew over the net I dove for it and smashed it back.

"Yo, Jess, it's only a game," Cami reminded me in a low voice.

But it wasn't a game anymore to me. It was everything. Somehow this dumb tennis game had grown into some kind of symbol for my whole messed-up family life. I wanted to pound Janie over the head with my tennis racket—and my dad too. But I couldn't. So I was going to settle for massacring them at tennis.

The volley continued for another couple of minutes, with everyone silent. I could hear my dad grunting as he made his shots. Janie's cheeks were pink with exertion. I was loving this.

After a series of hard hits on both sides, I tapped the ball lightly over the net. It dropped to the other side, just short of Janie's swing.

"Our advantage," I sang out. This felt great. I had never played so well in my life. One more point and the set would be ours. At one set each, we'd be tied.

Janie was ready to serve to Cami. But for some reason she wasn't serving. Then I saw that Cami was making funny faces at me, wiggling her eyebrows and jerking her head around as if she had water in her ear.

"I'm ready to serve, Cami, dear," came Janie's voice from the other side of the net.

I couldn't believe my ears. Janie had taken about a million years on her last serve, and now she had the nerve to tell Cami to hurry? I glared at her.

"Whenever you're ready, Cami," I said through clenched teeth. Janie looked away and patted her helmet hair into place.

Finally Janie served the ball. I hit it back to her. Cami caught my eye again and started making faces.

"What is your problem?" I whispered as Janie ran for the shot.

The ball was headed back toward me, over the net. I backed up to make the shot, so I couldn't hear Cami's whispered reply.

I smashed the ball hard but at a sharp angle. It just made it over the net. My father and Janie both dove for it—and missed.

*"Yeah!"* I yelled, waving my racket triumphantly.

"Nice game, girls," my father panted. "Okay, that's one set apiece. One more decides it."

I trotted over to Cami. "Come on, Cami. We can win this last set, I know it."

Cami looked at me. "Two things, Jess," she said in a low voice. *"Number one:* I think you're possessed. This is only tennis, remember? I hate to have to break it to you, but your dad is not the prize here. Whether you win or lose, Janie gets to keep him."

"I know, I know," I said, annoyed. "Look, I just want to beat them, okay? And I think we can do it. That last game—"

*"Number two,"* Cami interrupted. "I thought you might want to know that Danny is over there fixing the net on that court we were supposed to have."

"What?" I whirled around. There, right on the

next court, squatting down with his back to me and working on the net, was Danny. His back looked lean and strong in his green Golden's T-shirt, and his long dark hair fell forward toward his face, revealing a little bit of the back of his neck. I felt my knees go weak.

Then I panicked. What was I supposed to do? Should I call out to him? Had he seen me? He must have seen me when he walked out onto the court. After all, I was playing right next to him. But then why hadn't he said anything? Why was he ignoring me?

My stomach was in knots. I felt completely confused. Last night I had felt so close to Danny, but now I didn't know what to think.

My father's voice cut into my thoughts. "Okay, Janie, your serve. Last set; let's give it our best. We can't let the kids beat us, can we?"

I turned to Cami. I felt numb. "I don't want to play anymore," I said in a low voice.

Cami raised her eyebrows. "Are you kidding me? After the show you put on just now? There's no way they're going to let you out of it. Come on, just play." She jerked her head toward Danny. "He's not watching anyway."

"I know; that's the problem," I mumbled.

Cami gave me a sympathetic look.

"Hel-*lo*?" Janie called from across the court. "Are you serving now, girls? Maybe you want to spread out a little?"

I didn't even have the energy to hate her now. I

took my spot on the court as if I were in a trance.

Right after I served, I sneaked a look at Danny. He was still working on the net with his back to me. Janie's return flew right by me. I forgot to swing.

"Whoa, Jessie, wake up!" said my father. "What's happening, champ?"

"Love-fifteen." Janie announced the score.

I didn't answer. *Love,* I thought. *Love.* Danny had looked at me with love in his eyes the night before, I was sure of it.

I looked over at my father, standing there on the tennis court with a woman who was not my mother. My father had looked at my mother with love once too. But somehow his feelings had changed.

What if Danny's feelings about me changed too?

"Jess, it's your serve," Cami reminded me gently. She tossed me a ball.

Without even thinking, I served it over the net. Janie pounced on it. The ball was headed toward me, but it was a little short. I didn't feel like running.

Cami dove in front of me and just barely saved the shot. She glanced at me. "I can't play the whole game for both of us, you know, Jess," she joked.

But I didn't care about the game. Beating my dad and Janie didn't seem important anymore. All I could think about was Danny. I remembered the feel of his lips against mine. The way his hair had brushed against my cheek as he leaned in to kiss me. His eyes.

I wanted to run over to the next court and put my arms around him. But I was afraid. I'd never felt this way about anyone in my life. I'd die if Danny didn't feel the same way about me.

Besides, I hadn't told my father anything about Danny yet. What would he think if I suddenly threw myself on some strange boy?

I was only dimly aware of the game. I hit the ball when it came near me, but I missed more shots than I made. I didn't even know the score, how many games we had played.

A few minutes later, out of the corner of my eye, I saw Danny stand up. My heart beat faster. I turned to watch him, missing my shot.

Cami sighed as she retrieved the ball. "You've got it bad," she murmured.

I didn't say anything. My eyes were still on Danny. But he didn't turn around, didn't look at me. He just walked back toward the clubhouse—that slightly swaying, loping walk that made my heart melt.

The tennis ball came whizzing by me.

"Well, that's it," Janie announced with satisfaction in her voice. "Game, set, and match."

# NINE

I DIDN'T SEE Danny again for the rest of that day. Or the next day or the next day either. He didn't work at breakfast or any other meals, and I didn't spot him by the pool or the tennis courts. I spent the whole weekend asking myself questions—*What happened? Didn't our kiss mean anything to him? What about that look in his eyes? Why did he ignore me on the tennis court like that?* And most of all—*Where is he?*

If Danny was trying to avoid me, he was doing an awfully good job of it. I didn't see him once all weekend. It was as if he had just disappeared off the face of the earth.

Meanwhile Cami did her best to keep me busy. She made me go horseback riding, forced me to play tennis again (this time without Janie and my dad!), and talked me into getting a pedicure with her in the minispa. We even tried to go to the disco on Saturday night, but they wouldn't let us in because we were underage. On Sunday afternoon she insisted that I take a ride on a rowboat out on the lake with her and Kirk. I knew Cami was just trying to help, just trying to keep me from thinking about Danny. But it was no use.

I'd even asked Kirk about Danny when we were out on the boat, hoping that Kirk might know what was up. But Kirk only worked in the cocktail lounge part-time, three nights a week. The rest of the week he was a bartender at some tavern in town. He said he wasn't too sure who Danny was. Actually Kirk didn't seem too sure about much. He wasn't exactly talkative. He spent most of his time stroking his thin little goatee and grabbing at Cami. It didn't take long for me to start wishing I'd stayed back onshore.

By Sunday night I had pretty much narrowed the Danny-and-me scenario down to three possibilities.

*One:* He had once thought he cared about me, but then he had decided that what had happened between us was a mistake, and now he was doing his best to ignore and avoid me, hoping I would get the message.

*Two:* He had never cared about me at all, even in the beginning; the whole time he was just stringing me along, like he'd probably done to tons of girls at the hotel before me.

*Three:* He did care about me, at least a little, but it didn't matter because he'd been fired or quit his job, and I would never see him again anyway.

It almost didn't matter which one of these it was since they were all terrible. Of course I wanted to believe that Danny had cared for me, that his eyes had been telling me the truth, but what good was it if he was gone now?

Monday morning I slept through breakfast. Cami was out like a light. She'd been out really late riding around the woods in Kirk's car the night before. It didn't seem worth it to drag myself out of bed and rush over to the dining room with my dad and Janie on the chance that I might see Danny. After all, he hadn't worked in the dining room for a single meal in the past two and a half days.

At about ten o'clock Cami stretched, yawned loudly, and sat up in bed. I was already awake, staring at the ceiling and feeling rotten.

"Hey, Jess, listen. Do you want to go swimming with me and Kirk today?" she asked.

I rolled over to face her. "What? You mean at the pool?"

She shook her head. "Some quarry. It's in the woods somewhere. Kirk knows the place. He said it's where all the locals hang out."

For a moment my heart leaped. Maybe Danny went swimming there too. Then I stopped myself. I didn't even know if Danny *was* a "local," where he was from, anything about him. Besides, if Kirk had said he didn't know him, it wasn't likely that they hung out at the same places. And even if Danny was there, what would I do, wait for him to ignore me again like he had that day at the tennis courts?

"No, thanks," I told Cami. "I don't feel like it."

Cami looked concerned. "You okay, Jess?"

I nodded. "Yeah, I think I'll just hang out here. Relax and sit by the pool or something."

"Okay," said Cami. "I'll tell Kirk to forget about it."

"No, you go," I told her. "It's okay. I don't mind hanging out on my own for a while."

"Really?" Cami looked doubtful.

"Really," I assured her. In fact, the idea of spending some time by myself sounded kind of nice. I needed some time to relax, to get myself together, to get Danny out of my mind. Maybe I'd even take a walk on one of the trails, do a little exploring. The countryside up here was so different from down in Florida. At home everything was basically palm trees and more palm trees. It might be fun to hike into the woods here a little. I knew my dad and Janie had plans to play golf all day, so they wouldn't be bothering me. The more I thought about it, the more I liked the idea.

"Definitely. You go without me," I said to Cami.

An hour later I headed down a trail through the woods, a book and a rolled-up hotel towel under one arm and a bag with an apple and a bag of potato chips from the snack bar in my other hand. It was a hot day, clear and sunny, but the air on the shaded trail was cool and smelled like pine. I shivered just a little in my T-shirt and cutoffs.

I felt better than I had in days. Something about being on my own—away from my dad and Janie and even from Cami—was making it easier to leave behind my thoughts of Danny too. It reminded me of the

August before ninth grade, when all my friends had gone away and I was the only one left in South Beach.

At first I had hated it and felt incredibly lonely. I had started out taking my lunch and a book to the beach every day because I had nothing else to do. But after a couple of weeks I began to like it—sitting in my little spot in the shade behind an abandoned lifeguard stand, listening to the waves and the seagulls, munching on tuna sandwiches, and getting totally into my book. I read through a whole series that summer, these books about three friends who found a magic coin that let them travel through time. I loved them. By the end of the summer I felt like I knew those three characters practically better than my own real friends. I was almost sorry when everyone came back and school started again.

I didn't have too much hope for the book I had brought with me this time, though. It was some real-life mystery called *Grandma's Little Angels* that Janie had lent me a couple of days before. She said she knew one of the lawyers involved in the case the book was about and that it was a good story. Still, I was pretty sure I wasn't going to be too crazy about anything Janie was that enthusiastic about. It was the only book I had with me, though, so I figured I'd give it a chance.

I continued through the woods until I came to a small clearing covered with soft, brown pine needles. Patches of the lake were visible through the trees at the bottom of the hill below me. I spread out my towel and lay down on my stomach, gazing out at the slivers of sparkling water. I thought of Danny, of the walk we'd taken not too far from here that night. Then I put it out of my mind and opened *Grandma's Little Angels.*

Almost right away the book surprised me. It was much more interesting than I'd expected. And even though it was a real-life story, it was written like a novel. The story was about a kidnapping, and before I knew it, I was completely involved.

After I'd read about twenty pages, I realized that my legs were really itching me. I sat up and looked down at them. There were little mosquitoes hovering all around me, and I had a bunch of bites. The mosquitoes were obviously pretty active in the shady parts of the woods up here, even during the day. I'd picked the wrong place to settle down. Better head for someplace sunnier.

I tramped through the woods, still reading my book and eating my apple. A couple of times I almost tripped over some roots, but I was really into the book, and I didn't want to put it down. It was pretty suspenseful.

Suddenly the path emerged from the woods. I looked around and realized that I was headed toward the lake, from the opposite direction than the one Danny had taken me that night. To my right was the gazebo. I stared at it a moment, remembering, thinking. I swallowed hard. *Forget about it,* I told myself. *Forget about him.*

I decided the gazebo was as good a place as any to read. It was out of the woods, so the bugs wouldn't be too bad, but it was still shady, so it would be cool and comfortable. I threw my apple core into some bushes and headed through the grass toward the porchlike building.

Carefully I climbed the steps, avoiding the rotting parts. I crossed the gazebo floor and spread my towel out near the edge of the structure, by the lake. I lay down on my stomach and found my place in the book.

Soon I had forgotten about everything except what was happening in the story. I anxiously chewed on a fingernail and continued reading.

Suddenly there was a sound behind me, a creak in the floorboards. Startled, I whipped around. A dark shape was silhouetted against the sun on the lake. I gasped in fear and surprise.

"Jess?" said a familiar husky voice.

"Danny?" I shaded my eyes. I couldn't believe it.

He squatted down. I scrambled to sit up a little. We were both in the shade now, and I could see his face. He looked confused.

"Are you okay?" he asked.

I nodded, a little embarrassed. "It's just that I was reading this book, and I was at kind of a scary part. I guess you startled me."

"Oh." He shook his hair out of his eyes. "Sorry about that."

"That's okay."

Neither of us said anything for a few moments. We both looked out at the lake. I had a million questions to ask him, but I didn't know where to start.

I turned to face him. His eyes met mine. We sat

like that, our gazes locked, for what seemed like an eternity. I could feel my insides starting to melt, the world starting to fade away. His eyes seemed to say everything that he hadn't.

Danny moved forward and put his strong hands on my shoulders. He pulled me toward him gently and kissed me, softly at first and then more forcefully. I wrapped my arms around his neck and pressed my mouth to his. It felt so good to be with him again.

After a few moments Danny drew back. He looked at me tenderly and stroked my hair.

It took me a moment to find my voice.

"Where have you been?" I croaked at last.

Danny hesitated a moment, gazing off into space. I could tell he was thinking about something.

"I had to take care of a few things," he answered, his voice distant. He turned back to me, and our eyes met. He smiled. "But I'm back now."

He drew me toward him again and put his arms around me. His mouth was soft and warm, and I could feel his hands on my back through my T-shirt. I lost myself in the kiss.

Suddenly nothing mattered—none of it. Danny was back, and he cared about me. That much was clear.

And that was all I needed, for now.

# TEN

"WATCH OUT!" DANNY yelled.

I shielded my face from the splash as Danny cannonballed into the pool. He surfaced right beside where I was treading water and started to laugh.

"Oh, very funny!" I told him. "Here! Watch out your own self!" I splashed some water at his face.

"You want to fight, huh?" He pounded the surface of the water, drenching me. Then he dove underwater again.

I rubbed the water out of my eyes. I could see him circling me underwater. I let out a nervous giggle.

"Danny?" *What is he up to?*

Suddenly he shot out of the water behind me and grabbed my shoulders.

I shrieked.

He turned me around and took me in his arms, laughing. He kissed me, his face dripping with pool water. I kissed him back.

The past three days had been the happiest of my life. Since we had met at the gazebo on Monday, Danny and I had spent as much time as we could together, which was basically whenever he wasn't working. I still didn't know much more about him—we'd spent a lot more time kissing than we had talking—but I was more comfortable with him than I'd ever been with any boy in my life.

Our lips drew apart, and we stayed in each other's arms, the pool water gently lapping at our shoulders.

"You'd better behave yourself or I'll complain to the management," I teased. "I'll say you've been annoying the guests."

Danny glanced around at the nearly empty pool area. "What guests? Everyone's gone to their rooms to get dressed for dinner."

"What about me?" I joked. "I'm a guest here too, you know."

Danny's gaze dropped. He loosened his hold on me. "Yeah, I know," he said in a low voice.

"Danny?" I splashed a little water toward him. "I was just kidding. You realize that, right?" I said uneasily.

He swam away from me toward the ladder. "Yeah, sure. Anyway, I better go. I'm on the dinner shift."

"Oh, come on," I said. I swam after him. "Just stay in the pool with me a few more minutes," I coaxed.

He was already halfway up the ladder. He twisted to look at me. His body was dripping with water, and he had a hard expression on his face. "I *can't*, Jess. I have to work."

"Why are you so angry at me?" I asked him. "I

only said it because I want to be with you."

"Well, I want to be with you too," he responded. His face reddened. "Do you think I *want* to go clear away people's dirty dishes for two hours? That I like handing out towels all day? That I enjoy working four jobs at once here?"

I stared at him in astonishment. Normally Danny seemed so calm, so reserved. I'd never heard an outburst like that from him. I could tell he was really upset.

He sat on the side of the pool and put his head in his hands. I climbed out and sat beside him.

"Forget it, Jess," Danny said, his head still in his hands. "We're from two different worlds. You're here to have fun, to play tennis with your family. I'm just the guy who fixes the net."

"Is that what this is all about?" I asked in amazement. "I get it. *That's* why you acted like you didn't notice me that day on the courts!"

He looked up at me. "*Me?* You were the one who was so into your game that you didn't even see me. I felt invisible, like I was just part of the equipment to you."

Now I was angry. "Danny," I said, fixing my eyes directly on him, "I wanted to see you more than anything that day. You've got to believe me. Okay, maybe I didn't notice you at first. But it's not like you think. I'm not just some spoiled little tennis snob who can't be bothered to take time away from her game. There was a lot going on that day. A lot of bad family stuff. Stuff with my dad and his disgusting girlfriend."

Danny took my hand. "I'm sorry. It was wrong of me to judge you like that. I know you're not a snob. I guess I'm just under a lot of pressure lately. There's a lot of stuff going on for me too."

"Maybe you're working too hard here," I said gently. "Maybe it's too tough to try hold down so many jobs at once."

He turned to me. "I have no choice," he said solemnly. "I'm going to turn eighteen in November, and I have to earn as much as I can before then."

"Why?" I asked him. "Why before you turn eighteen?"

He hesitated, his eyes fixed on mine.

"Nothing," he said softly. "Forget it." He gave me one of those little half smiles. "Like I said, you and I are from two different worlds. It's like you're from Mercury and I'm from . . . Pluto."

I wanted to ask him more, but he tilted my face up toward his and kissed me before I could say a word.

Afterward he looked down at me tenderly. He was smiling, but something in his eyes was sad. Something that kept me from asking any more questions.

"Well, maybe so," I murmured. "But I get a pretty good feeling we might be able to meet on some planet in between."

Ten minutes later I hurried down the path toward the Mercury bungalow, my hair still dripping from the pool and a towel wrapped around my waist. As I rushed by the front entrance on my way to the back, the door opened.

"Jess?" my father called out. "Is that you?"

"Yeah, Dad, hi!" I called back.

My father came to the door. "Jessica, come in here for a moment, please."

"What?" I said, a little defensively. My father hardly ever called me "Jessica," and when he did, it was never good.

"I asked you to come in," my father repeated. "I'd like to speak to you about something."

This definitely didn't sound good at all.

"Can't I just have a shower first?" I asked, stalling. "I have to get ready for dinner."

"That is one of the things I want to talk to you about," said my father. "Now come in here, please."

From the tone of his voice I knew there was no getting out of this one. I walked reluctantly toward the door.

"Janie and I have been ready to go to the dining room and waiting for you for twenty minutes," my father said before I'd even gotten inside. "We asked Cami where you were, and she didn't seem to have any idea."

I stepped inside the room. Janie was perched on the edge of the bed, looking prim as usual in one of her pastel-colored getups and pink lipstick. The room smelled like hair spray, so I could tell she'd been working on her helmet. She had an annoyed, expectant look on her face, and her hands were folded neatly in her lap. Her whole appearance made me want to charge at her and tackle her to the ground.

"Oh, Jess, there you are," Janie said in her best icicle-coated voice.

I ignored her and turned to my father. "Dad, can I shower now?"

"Not until I have my say," my father responded. "Jessica, you know we always go to dinner at six. This is very inconsiderate."

I glared at him. It was bad enough that he was getting mad at me over this, but to do it in front of Janie was totally humiliating.

"Okay, fine, I was a little late," I said through clenched teeth. "I'm sorry." I headed for the door that connected their room to mine and Cami's.

"That's not all." My father's voice stopped me in my tracks. "I'd like to know just what you've been up to for the past few days."

"Up to?" I tried to make my voice sound innocent. "What do you mean?"

"Jess, you might as well tell the truth," Janie said.

"And *you* might as well stay out of this!" I snapped back.

"Jessica!" My father's voice was harsh.

"My life is none of her business!" I was practically crying now. "She's not my mother!"

"Well, I *am* your father. And I'd like to know where you've been spending all your time lately," said my father. "Just who is this boy Janie says she saw you with behind the stables yesterday?"

I froze. I'd meant to tell my dad about Danny, eventually. I just hadn't gotten around to it. At least that's what I'd been saying to myself. But the truth was I wasn't that eager to tell my dad at all. I was a little ashamed to admit it, but I wasn't sure how he'd feel about my going out with someone who worked at the hotel, how he'd react. Besides, what Danny and I had felt was so special that part of me just wanted to keep it private. The last thing I wanted was for my dad to ask a million questions and come up with a bunch of rules about when and where I could see Danny.

It figured that Janie would have to go and ruin everything. I could just imagine what it was she had seen. Danny had been working there, feeding the horses, and I'd stopped by to see him. We'd stolen a couple of minutes together behind the building and ended up in each other's arms. Janie must have come along at just the right—or wrong—moment.

I shot Janie a furious look. Not only was she butting into my life, but now she was a tattletale too. I bet she'd just loved running to my father with the information that she'd seen me locking lips with someone behind the stables.

"Jess, I certainly hope you realize that I only mentioned that to your father for your own good," Janie said in her fake-sweet voice.

"That's right," said my father. "We're concerned about you. If something's going on in your life, I want to know about it."

"Oh, yeah, sure," I said, really angry now. "If you cared so much about what was going on in my life, why did you move out like that? Why did you leave?" My voice was cracking.

My father's face crumpled a little. I could tell I had hurt him with what I had said. But I didn't care. After all, he had hurt me too.

"Jess, the divorce was something that happened between me and Mom," he said carefully.

"That's right. You had nothing to do with it," Janie put in.

"Yeah, but *you* had everything to do with it!" I yelled at her. I turned to my father. I was trying desperately to blink back the tears. The last thing I wanted was to break down in front of Janie. "I've got news for you, Dad. I lived in that house too. When you left Mom, you also left me!"

"Jess," my father tried, "I know I hurt you. But I'm still your father."

"You could have fooled me!" I shot back. "This is such a joke, the way you're acting like you suddenly care about me, about who I'm seeing and what I'm doing. You don't know anything about me at all!" I stormed across the room toward the door.

"All right, now, let's all just calm down," said Janie. "Jess, if you move quickly, we can all still make it to dinner."

"Forget it. I'm not going!" I cried. "Just go without me. I'm not hungry anyway!" I pulled open the door and stormed into my room, slamming the door behind me.

Cami was sitting on the bed, painting her toenails orange. She looked up when I came in. "Sorry about that. I tried to cover for you."

"It's not your fault." I sank down on my bed and let out a deep breath of air. "I can't stand them," I said angrily. I turned to her. "You don't know how lucky you are that your parents leave you alone and let you do whatever you want."

Cami shrugged. "I guess. Still, sometimes I wonder

what it would be like to have someone care about you enough to argue with you about stuff like that."

I looked at her. I'd never heard Cami say anything like that. I'd just assumed she liked the way things were in her house. I'd always envied her freedom. It had never occurred to me that she might not appreciate it as much as I imagined.

"What do you think of this color?" Cami asked, abruptly changing the subject. She stuck out her foot. "Is it going to clash with my red pants?"

"Probably," I informed her.

"Good." She grinned. "That's just the effect I'm going for."

I laughed. Cami could always cheer me up, usually without even trying. "Are you going out?"

She shrugged. "Kirk didn't say anything. But I've got a feeling he might show up."

"You know, you can go to dinner with them if you want," I told her. "You don't have to hide out here with me just because I threw a fit."

"Mmmm, let's see. Dinner alone with Janie and Peter? Thanks, but I think I'll skip it," she replied.

"I guess Danny will probably wonder where I am," I said, thinking.

"I've got an idea," said Cami. "Why don't I go over there and see if I can find him? I'll tell him what happened. Maybe he can even slip me some food to bring back here."

"I don't know, Cami," I said. "I don't want you to get him in trouble or anything."

"Don't worry about it," she answered. "I'll

sneak in the kitchen entrance and look for him. No one will even notice. Piece of cake. Or would you rather have pie?"

I laughed. "Anything. I'm starved."

"No problem," Cami said. "You hop in the shower, and I'll be back in a few minutes."

"Okay," I said. "And Cami, tell him . . ." I stopped. *Tell him what?* I thought. *That I've only been away from him for twenty minutes and I miss him already? That I can't wait until we're together again? That I'm pretty sure I'm falling in love with him?* "Oh, nothing," I said finally.

Cami grinned. "Don't worry, Jess. I'll make sure he gets the message."

A little while later Cami returned with the food—some cold chicken, biscuits wrapped in napkins, and a whole chocolate cake in a box! I sat at the table in our room in my long white summer nightgown, my freshly washed hair wrapped up in a towel, and we set out the food.

"That was a pretty close call," Cami reported. "I almost bumped into your dad and Janie on the path coming out of the dining room on my way back. I had to hide behind a tree so they wouldn't see me with all this food." I was afraid they might decide to prosecute me for aiding and abetting a tantrum thrower."

I laughed. "What about Danny?" I asked her. "What did you tell him?"

"I said you'd been locked up in a dungeon by an evil warlock," she said. "I told him the warlock's spell would probably keep you here all night but that you'd look for him tomorrow at breakfast. He was pretty busy running around, though. He didn't really have time to talk." She smiled. "He made a special trip to nab the cake, though. He seems so nice, Jess."

"He is, Cami," I told her, feeling a smile come to my face.

"Hey, you guys can hang out with me and Kirk sometime," she said enthusiastically. "How about the Fourth of July barbecue? You know, the party with the fireworks over by the lake? I think Kirk's working there that night. What about Danny?"

"I don't know," I answered. "I'll ask him."

Just then we were interrupted by a splattering sound against the window.

"What's that?" I asked.

Cami twisted in her seat. There was another splatter. "Someone's throwing pebbles," she said. She turned to me and grinned. "See? I told you Kirk would probably show up."

She stood up and walked to the door. When she opened it, a gust of cool night mountain air came in. I watched as Cami peered out into the dark.

"Kirk?" she whispered. "Where are you?"

I could barely hear a murmured response from outside.

"Okay, just a sec," Cami responded. She turned back to me. "Hey, Jess, this one's for you."

"For me? What do you mean?" I stood up and walked to the door.

Danny stood outside on the path. With a little

gasp I hurried out to meet him, my bare feet smarting on the sharp pebbles of the path. I took his hand and pulled him into the shadows.

"What are you doing here?" I whispered.

"I wanted to make sure you were okay," he said. "Your friend said you were in some kind of trouble."

"Oh, it was just a fight with my dad," I explained. I glanced around quickly. "And I'm afraid it's going to turn into an even bigger one if he finds me out here like this."

"Okay, no problem," said Danny. "I just wanted to see you, that's all. I was afraid I might not get a chance to talk to you tomorrow."

"What do you mean—why not?" I asked.

"I have to go somewhere for the day," he told me. "I've got some stuff I have to do."

"You're going away again?" I said incredulously.

"I have to," he said. He squeezed my hand. "I'll be back tomorrow night, though."

*"Jess."* Cami's urgent whisper came through the darkness from the door of the bungalow. "Jess, hurry!"

"What is it?" I whispered back.

"Your dad just knocked on the door," she said. "I told him you were in the bathroom. He'll probably be back any minute."

"I'd better get inside," I said to Danny.

"Okay, go." He gave me a quick kiss. "Tomorrow night. Meet me at the gazebo at nine o'clock, okay?" He squeezed my hand again.

"Okay." Once again my mind was full of questions. But once again they were going to have to wait.

# ELEVEN

I T RAINED ALL the next day, which was Thursday, and all night. Cami and I stayed in our room for most of the morning, reading and eating the rest of Danny's cake. Shortly before lunch there was a knock on the door from my dad and Janie's room.

Cami and I exchanged glances. I hadn't spoken to my father or Janie since our argument the night before. By the time my dad had come into to our room again after Danny had left, Cami and I were both in bed, pretending to be asleep.

But I knew I couldn't avoid my father forever. Besides, as long as Cami was there with me it couldn't be too bad, right?

"Come in," I called. The door opened.

"Hello, girls," said my father, a little stiffly. "Cami, I wonder if you'd mind taking your magazine into the other room for a moment with Janie? I'd like to talk to Jessie in private."

*Oh, well,* I thought, *there goes my protection.*

Cami stood up. "Oh, sure, Mr. G. No problem." She made a quick Janie-pursed-lips face at me as she headed for the door.

I tried not to smile. I was sure Janie was going to be just as thrilled about this arrangement as Cami.

My father turned to me as Cami closed the door. "I was very disturbed by what happened last night."

I stared down at my lap. "I know, Dad. Me too."

"This isn't easy for any of us," he went on. "Believe me, I feel anguish every day over what I've done to your life and to your mother's too."

I looked up in surprise. "You do?"

"Of course," he said, sitting down on the bed beside me. "You may not realize this, but there were a lot of problems between Mom and me long before Janie came along." He sighed. "I couldn't keep living a lie."

"But didn't you love Mom?" I asked him. "What happened? How could you just fall out of love like that?"

He shook his head. "I don't know what to say. Nobody knows exactly why these things happen." He took my hand. "But I do know that I never wanted to hurt you. I realize how angry you are about all this, and I'm sorry, honey."

"Oh, Dad!" I threw myself into his arms and burst into tears. "I just wish things could be the way they were," I said, my voice a little muffled by his shoulder.

He held my shoulders and looked me in the face. "I know, but they can't. You have to accept that now. Mom and I are starting new lives. I'm going to marry Janie, and your mother's beginning a new career. But Jess, no matter what we're doing, what's going on in your life will always be important to us. To both of us."

I nodded and sniffed a little.

My father grinned. "So who's the lucky guy anyway? How did this big romance start without my hearing anything about it?"

I shrugged. "His name's Danny, Dad. Danny Jordan."

My father nodded encouragingly. "And? Is he staying here with his family? Where's he from?"

"Actually he works here," I explained.

My father looked a little surprised. "Works here? Oh, you mean like a summer job?"

"Um, yeah, that's right," I said. This was the tough part. I was pretty sure my dad wouldn't like it if he realized how little I actually knew about Danny. "His family lives in the area," I fibbed. "In Deer Creek."

"You mean Deer Falls?"

I forced a laugh. "Did I say Deer Creek? I meant Deer Falls. Anyway, that's where he's from."

"Okay, well, next time you're going to see him, I'd like to meet him," said my father.

I hesitated. I wasn't about to tell my father that the next time I planned to see Danny was that night down at the gazebo by the lake. And I wasn't sure how I felt about the idea of my dad meeting Danny at all. My father was sure to ask him a bunch of questions, and I knew for myself how funny Danny was about stuff like that. And my dad wasn't the type to back off when someone seemed reluctant to talk. In fact, it would probably just send him into high-gear lawyer mode. From what I knew of Danny, he definitely wouldn't appreciate being cross-examined. The more I thought about it, the more it seemed like a good idea to put this meeting off as long as possible.

"Um, okay, Dad. Sure. Whatever," I said. I tried to think of a way to change the subject. "So I guess it's about lunchtime, huh?"

My father glanced at his watch. "Looks that way. Before we go, though, there's one other thing I wanted to talk to you about."

"What is it?" I asked.

"It's Janie," he said. "I'd like you to give her a little more of a chance."

I squirmed uncomfortably. I couldn't stand Janie. Couldn't he see that? I didn't know what to say.

My father cleared his throat. "I realize it's a difficult situation, Jessica."

*Oh, no,* I thought. *Here we go with the "Jessica" stuff again.*

"But I'd like you to understand that Janie is in no way trying to take Mom's place," he continued. "The thing is, I know you two could get along very well if you just got to know each other better. You're a lot more alike than you think."

"Me and Janie?" I said incredulously. *He must be out of his mind.*

"That's right," he replied. "Janie's a lot smarter than you realize. She's a top-notch lawyer who's handled more than her share of very difficult cases.

Family law is not an easy area, you know. There are a lot of heightened emotions when a family is in crisis over divorce or custody or whatever. Dealing with it can be like navigating your way through a minefield."

I looked at him. Was he actually saying these things to me? *He* was telling *me* that there were a lot of strong feelings involved when families broke up? And he expected me to believe that *Janie* was some kind of "family superwoman" who came flying in to save the day?

"Well, anyway, I'd just like you to think about it," my father finished. "So, what do you say we get those two from the other room and go over to lunch? I think Janie packed an umbrella. Maybe we can all huddle under it and make it over to the main building without getting too wet."

It continued raining off and on for the rest of the day and into the evening. Cami and I stayed in the main building for the afternoon, playing Ping-Pong until it was dinnertime. It let up a little while we were eating, but by the time the four of us made our way back to the bungalow, it was pouring again.

Later, in our room, Cami turned to me. "It's raining pretty hard, Jess. Are you still going?"

I glanced at the clock. Eight-thirty. I had promised to meet Danny at the gazebo at nine, and I wasn't about to let the rain stop me.

"I want to, but I wonder if he'll show up," I said. "What if he thinks I'm not coming because of the rain?"

"Good point," said Cami. "Kirk canceled on *me* because of the rain." She let out a scornful little laugh. "Not that I see what the rain had to do with it. We were supposed to play pool together over in the main building." She shrugged. "No big deal, though. I was starting to get a little tired of him anyway."

"Really?" I was surprised. "I thought you guys were getting along well. He definitely seemed pretty into you when we were all out on the rowboat that day."

"I guess," she said. "But Kirk's kind of a baby. Believe me, older doesn't necessarily mean more mature." She grinned. "He's got this really cute friend I met the other night, though. His name's Dean."

I shook my head. "You are amazing, Cami." I crossed the room and peered out the window. "Hey, maybe it's letting up," I said hopefully. Unfortunately I didn't have an umbrella.

Cami laughed. "Even if it isn't, it's pretty obvious that you're going. What do you want me to tell your dad if he checks?"

"I don't know," I answered. Most evenings my dad and Janie left the bungalow. They met friends for drinks at the bar or they went to see the show at the cabaret in the main building. But I had the feeling the rain was going to keep them in tonight. Cami waved a hand at me. "Don't worry, I'll think of something."

I checked the clock on the night table. Ten of nine. It was now or never. I grabbed my jean jacket, the only jacket I had brought with me on the trip, and slipped it on over my white hooded sweatshirt and long green-and-white-flowered skirt.

"See you later," I said to Cami as I opened the door and stepped out.

The rain was still pretty heavy. I pulled the hood of my sweatshirt over my head and hurried down the muddy path toward the lake.

*This is crazy,* I told myself as I dodged huge mud puddles on the path. *He probably isn't even coming.* The shoulders of my jean jacket were already soaked, and my skirt stuck to my legs as I walked. In a matter of minutes I was shivering. I felt as if I had jumped in the pool with all my clothes on. The rain ran in little rivers down my face, and the sweatshirt hood was plastered to my head.

As I emerged from the woods near the lake I didn't have much hope of seeing Danny. I tried to console myself with the fact that I'd probably see him working at breakfast the next morning. After all, I couldn't expect him to come out to meet me in this weather.

But when I turned the corner to approach the gazebo, he was there! I couldn't believe it. I ran the rest of the way, and Danny turned around just as I got there, his face lighting up when he saw me. I ran up the steps. He opened his arms, and I threw myself into them. We hugged. I buried my wet head in his shoulder. He felt warm.

I leaned back slightly to look at him. He was pretty wet too. He was wearing a Windbreaker, but his head was bare, and his dark hair was dripping. I smiled.

"I can't believe you came," he said.

"I had to," I replied.

He nodded. "Me too."

We kissed. Correction: We *tried* to kiss, but my teeth were chattering so badly that we had to stop.

"Oh, wow, you're freezing," he said. He took my hand. "Come on."

I ran back out into the rain with him. "Where are we going?" I yelled.

"My truck!" he yelled back. "It's parked up the road. We'll go to my room!"

I hesitated a moment. Was this a good idea? What if my father found out?

Danny paused to look at me. "Jessie, you've got to dry off," he pointed out.

I nodded. "Okay, show me the way."

Danny led me up a short path to a clearing, where an old red pickup truck was parked. He opened the passenger door for me and I got in. Soon we were bouncing along a dirt road that headed off in the opposite direction from the main building and the Galaxy Circle bungalows. After a couple of minutes we came to a row of plain, one-story wooden buildings. They were identical, painted a drab brown, each with a number above the front door and a row of unornamented rectangular windows along the sides.

"These are the 'barracks,'" Danny said softly as we got out of the truck. "Staff housing." He led me toward a building marked 5 and pointed to a dark window at the far end. "That's mine. Come on."

We hurried inside, and I followed Danny down a drab hallway to a corner door that said 5-C. He fished in the pocket of his Windbreaker for a key and opened the door. I followed him inside.

There was nothing particularly remarkable about the room. In fact, there weren't really any personal touches at all, other than a candle stuck into an empty Coke bottle on the dresser and an acoustic guitar leaning against the wall by the bed. The only other items in the room were the single bed, covered with a rumpled blue blanket; a worn easy chair in the corner; and the dresser, which was bare except for the candle, a Walkman, and a bunch of coins. There were no photographs, no posters on the walls, no books, no papers, nothing. It was kind of hard to believe that anyone lived there at all.

"Is this really your room?" I asked him in surprise. If I was looking for clues to Danny's life, I certainly wasn't going to find any there.

"Yeah." He pulled open a dresser drawer and began rummaging through the clothes inside. "I would have brought you here before, but the barracks are technically off-limits to anyone but employees. I didn't want to take the chance during the day. Here." He tossed me a pair of sweatpants and a rumpled flannel shirt. "They'll be a little big, but at least you'll be dry. I'll get us some towels."

Danny left the room, and I changed my clothes. The sweatpants were okay once I pulled the drawstring tight, although they were a little long. The flannel shirt fit more like a nightgown, but it smelled like Danny, and it felt wonderful. I rolled up the sleeves and sat down on the bed.

Danny came back with two towels. He tossed one to me and rubbed his head with the other. "Feel better?"

"Much," I answered. I toweled my hair and tried to run my fingers through it a bit. It was damp and snarled.

"Here, let me." Danny sat down beside me on the bed. Gently and carefully he started to work his way through my tangles with his hands.

"Mmmm, that feels nice," I said dreamily. "And it doesn't even hurt. How'd you get so good at this?"

"Practice," he answered.

I turned to face him. "Oh, really? Practice on who?"

He grinned. "On my *sisters*. When they were little, they both had really long, curly hair. It used to get incredibly tangled. My mom was always threatening to give them haircuts if it got to be too much trouble. I used to help Lisa and Lila comb it out at night."

"Lisa and Lila, huh? What's your mom's name, Lola?" I joked, turning my back toward him again.

"Almost." He smiled. "Lena."

"No!" I said. "Really? That's incredible. So where are they all now?"

Danny's hands stopped moving. He took them out of my hair. "My mother's dead," he said in a low voice.

I whirled around. "Oh, Danny, no! Really?"

He didn't have to answer. The answer was right there in his eyes.

"D-Danny," I stammered, staring down at

my hands. "I'm really sorry. I didn't know."

"It's okay," he said softly. "I know you didn't. It happened five years ago, when I was twelve." He paused. "I don't really like to talk about it that much."

"Okay, I understand," I said quickly. I didn't know what to do. I felt awkward, like I had said something terrible.

Then I looked at Danny's face. He was staring off into space, at a spot just beyond my shoulder. It was obvious that he was hurting. His eyes were full of pain, and a little muscle in his jaw was twitching.

I reached out and stroked his cheek as gently as I could. He shifted his gaze, and his eyes met mine. At the exact same moment we moved forward to kiss each other.

"Oh, Jess," he murmured into my hair.

"Danny," I whispered back. "Danny, I—"

I stopped myself, realizing what I'd been about to say. The words had almost flown out of my mouth on their own. Quickly I put my mouth against his, willing the words back down my throat, burying them deep down in my chest.

I wasn't ready. Not yet. I *did* love Danny, I knew that. But I wasn't ready to tell him, to trust him with my heart completely. At least not until he was ready to trust me with more. Even though Danny had revealed a part of himself to me tonight, had told me something personal and painful, I knew there was more. Things he still wasn't telling me.

And I couldn't help feeling hurt by that.

# TWELVE

THE FOLLOWING MORNING I walked into the dining area with my father, Janie, and Cami and scanned the large room for Danny. He'd told me the night before that he'd be working the breakfast shift.

Somehow the time had flown by, the night before. It only seemed like we'd been kissing for a few minutes, but by the time we removed our arms from around each other, it was after midnight. I'd gotten this panicky feeling, wondering if my dad had checked the room and found me gone.

But everything had turned out okay. The rain had stopped by the time Danny walked me back to the bungalow, my wet clothes in a bundle under my arm. We'd forced ourselves to say good night quickly, and when I got inside, Cami informed me that my dad hadn't knocked on the door once all night. I breathed a sigh of relief and went to bed, happy and exhausted, curling up in Danny's big flannel shirt.

I knew Danny must be feeling as tired as I was. He'd probably gotten to bed later than I had, and I knew he had to report to the kitchen at seven-thirty in the morning.

The hostess showed us to a table, which was, by some miracle, empty.

"This is nice," Janie said as we took our seats. "We don't have to sit with anyone else."

I looked at her in surprise. "I thought you liked eating family style."

"It can be fun, but I don't mind taking a break now and then either," she responded. She smiled guiltily. "Especially first thing in the morning. A personality like Herb Relleck's can be a little hard to take before I've had my coffee."

"Speaking of coffee, I'd like some right away," said my father. "And a little breakfast to go with it." He waved his hand. "Excuse me, we'd like to order."

"Um, your waiter will be with you in a minute, sir," said a familiar voice.

I looked up, startled. It was Danny. He must have been passing by when my dad decided to flag him down. Our eyes met for a moment, and then we both looked away.

"Oh, hello, there," Janie said. "Don't we know you? Or rather, doesn't *Jess* know you?"

"Never a dull moment around here," Cami murmured into her napkin.

I stared down at my plate and swallowed. This was so weird. I'd only seen Danny at a couple of meals before, and he hadn't ever actually serviced our table—not since that first day, with the orange juice. We'd always just managed to make eye contact across the room and exchange a quick smile now and then. And since my dad and Janie had no idea who he was, no one had noticed. But I should have realized that Janie's seeing us at the stables that day would mean the end of that.

My father looked confused. "What are you talking about, Janie?"

Danny wiped his hand on his jeans and extended it toward my father. "I'm Danny Jordan, Mr. Graham. I'm Jess's . . . friend."

"Oh?" said my father, then an expression of realization crossed his face. "Oh!" He stood up slightly and shook Danny's hand. "Nice to meet you, young man." He gestured toward the table. "Won't you join us?"

I felt my face flush. "*Dad,* he has to work."

"Oh, right," my father said. "How silly of me. Of course. Well, maybe another time. I'd like to get to know you a little better."

"Sure, okay." Danny nodded. "Well, I guess I'll get your waiter now." He walked away.

We all sat there in uncomfortable silence for a moment or two. I guess no one knew what to say.

Finally Cami picked up the little card from the table that listed upcoming events and activities at the hotel. "Oh, would you look at this! There's a croquet tournament this afternoon."

"Do you *play* croquet, Cami?" Janie asked.

"Not really, but I bet I could pick it up pretty quick," Cami answered. "After all, how much could there be to it, just whacking a little ball through a hoop with a hammer, right?"

"Actually it's a little more complicated than that," Janie said.

"Janie grew up in Canada," my father explained. "Her high school had a croquet team up there."

"We were regional champions," Janie put in.

"You must be proud," said Cami.

I covered my mouth with my napkin and tried not to laugh. I could tell that Janie had no idea whether Cami was joking or not.

"So maybe croquet's out." Cami looked back at the card in her hands. "Okay, here's something I'm good at—'Shopping Trip.' Want to go, Jess? It says there's a bus leaving this morning for a mall near here."

"Okay," I said. Shopping sounded like fun. I knew Danny would be working at the stables after breakfast anyway. He had a couple of hours free before dinner, and we'd promised to meet at the boathouse near the lake at four.

"Great," Cami said. "I could use some new stuff. I'm starting to get really bored with all the clothes I brought up here with me."

I laughed. "Cami, only you could get bored with leopard-print tops and sequined sneakers."

I heard someone laugh across the table and

looked up. To my surprise, it was Janie. I was amazed. I didn't think I'd ever seen Janie laugh before. Could it be possible that she was actually developing a sense of humor—about *Cami?*

Later that morning Cami and I stood in front of a store called Cookie's at the mall, scanning the window display of Easter-egg-colored jogging suits with pictures of baby animals painted on the fronts.

"Boy, talk about a sugar overload," Cami said. "This is making me feel nauseous. Who would ever wear stuff like this?"

"Actually—" I began.

"Don't answer that," she cut me off. "I know what you're going to say. And I agree. Janie definitely should have come along on this shopping trip. This mall has the worst clothes I've ever seen."

"Hey, I think this could be a new look for you, Cami," I teased.

"Oh, yeah, right," Cami cracked. "I could show up at school in September with a whole new image—toddler chic." She laughed.

I was silent. The mention of September made me think of only one thing—the fact that Danny and I would have to leave each other before the end of the summer. Even though it was still a while away, I was already dreading it. How would I say good-bye? Would I ever see him again?

Cami put her hand on my shoulder. "Hey, Jess," she said gently. "Don't think about it. Try to just live for the moment."

I nodded, even though I knew that was impossible.

"And speaking of the moment, at this moment I happen to be hungry," Cami announced. "How much time do we have before the bus leaves to go back to the hotel?"

I checked my watch. "Half an hour."

"I saw a pizza place back there," she said. "Let's go get a slice."

"Okay, sure," I said.

We turned to walk back through the mall.

"Hey!" a voice called out from behind us. "I know you!"

We turned around. Standing behind us was a tall guy in a black T-shirt and jeans with shaggy dark hair.

"Dean!" Cami exclaimed. "Hi!"

The guy grinned. "You're from Golden's. Kirk's friend, right?"

"Well, sort of," she said. "This is my friend Jessica."

"Hey." He nodded. He turned to Cami. "So what are you up to?"

"Not too much." Cami shrugged. "Just hanging out. Mostly we just had to get away from the hotel. It gets so boring."

"I've been over there a couple times," said Dean. "Looked pretty nice to me. They got a pool and everything."

"Well, you should come again sometime," Cami said. She winked. "We could go for a swim or something."

Dean nodded eagerly. "Yeah, sounds good. Maybe I will."

"Actually," Cami said with a gleam in her eye, "there's a big party happening Sunday for the Fourth of July. Fireworks over the lake and everything." She looked up through her eyelashes and added, "It should be very romantic."

I smiled. Watching Cami in action was amazing. I never could have said something like that to a boy I barely knew.

And, of course, it worked.

"Sounds great," Dean said enthusiastically. "Sunday, huh? What time?"

"I'm not sure exactly when it starts, but I'm sure the real fun will begin after sunset," she replied. "Tell you what, why don't you meet me outside the main building at eight o'clock?"

Dean grinned. "You got it. See you then. Hey, nice to meet you, Ginny."

I didn't bother to correct him. I knew it wasn't really his fault he'd gotten my name wrong. It was pretty much what was to be expected when Cami cast one of her spells on a guy. I guess being around her was just so overpowering that Dean didn't have any brain cells left to use for anything else.

Dean walked away, and Cami grinned at me. "Mission accomplished."

"But Cami, I thought Kirk was supposed to be at that party," I pointed out.

She waved a hand in the air. "Like I said, I'm getting tired of him. Besides, he'll be busy bartending, and I want to have fun. Are you and Danny going together?"

"I forgot to ask him," I told her. I glanced at my watch. "Hey, it's twelve-twenty. We only have ten minutes till the bus leaves. We'd better hurry if you still want that slice."

We rushed the rest of the way to the pizza place. But when we got there, the man behind the counter frowned at us.

"We don't sell slices," he said. "Just whole pies."

"Okay, fine, give me a pie," Cami said.

I stared at her. "Are you crazy? We'll never be able to eat all that."

She shrugged. "We'll give the rest away. Or leave it here." She turned to the pizza man. "Could you hurry, please? We've got a bus to catch."

By the time the pizza was ready, it was twelve twenty-nine.

"Come on!" Cami yelled, throwing money on the counter. "We can eat it on the bus." She grabbed the pizza box.

We ran to the parking lot and got there just in time to see the bus leaving.

"Wait! Wait!" Cami yelled.

"Forget it. We missed it," I told her. I shook my head. "This is great. How are we supposed to get back now?"

"Let's figure it out after lunch," Cami said cheerfully. She sat down on the curb.

"What are you doing?"

"Eating. I'm *hungry*." She opened the box and pulled out a piece of pizza. "Want one?"

"Sure." I laughed. "Why not?" I sat down beside her.

We were silent for a couple of minutes, chewing. A few people walking by stared at us.

"I guess we're going to have to hitch back," said Cami.

"I wonder if the police are strict about that stuff up here," I said.

Cami grinned. "Well, at least if we get arrested, we know where we can find a couple of good lawyers in the area."

Just then a green pickup truck pulled up in front of us. Inside were two guys wearing Golden's hats. One of them stuck his head out the window. He looked kind of familiar. After a moment I recognized him as the young-looking guy with the electric hedge clippers who had been staring at Cami that day at the pool. The man in the driver's seat was older, wearing a baseball cap and chewing on a cigar.

"Excuse me, aren't you staying at Golden's?" the younger one asked.

"That's right!" I said, relieved. "You work there, don't you?"

"Perfect!" Cami declared. "Can you give us a ride?"

"Sure, no problem." The younger guy got out. He stared at Cami for a second and then looked down at his feet. "You can probably both fit in here. Might be a bit of a squeeze."

"What about you?" I asked. "Where are you going to sit?"

121

"Oh, I'll ride in the back," he answered.

"The back? That sounds like fun," Cami said. "I'll hop back there too."

The guy blushed a little bit. "Well, okay, if you're sure."

"Here, I'll hold the pizza box," I volunteered. Cami handed it to me.

The younger guy climbed up into the back of the truck and bashfully held out his hand to help Cami in. His face was bright red.

I got in front with the old guy, who nodded at me before pulling out of the parking lot.

Twenty minutes later we arrived back at the hotel parking lot by the main building.

"Thanks a lot," I said to the driver. He nodded again without looking at me. I got out of the truck and watched as the boy in the back scrambled to help Cami down.

He shuffled his feet in the dirt a little and stuck his hands in his pockets. "Okay, bye now," he said finally.

The driver beeped the horn. The younger guy climbed back into the truck's cab, stumbling a little as he stared at Cami.

"Bye-bye!" Cami sang out. "Thanks for the ride!"

I turned to her as the truck drove away. "Boy, Cami, that guy really likes you."

"Who, Quentin?" she said. "Yeah, he's a cute guy. You're not going to believe what he told me about Kirk, though."

"What's that?" I asked.

"Kirk's married and has a kid!"

"What?" I said, astonished. "That's awful!"

"Well, Quentin said they're separated. Kirk's wife is Quentin's aunt," she explained. "Kirk doesn't live with her and the kid anymore. But still, it's pretty amazing that Kirk never mentioned that little detail to me, don't you think?"

"I think it's terrible," I told her. "How could he keep something like that a secret from you?"

But as I said it, the words stuck in my throat. Danny was keeping things from me too. I was almost sure of it. Not that I thought Danny was *married* or anything. That was too ridiculous. But there was still no denying the fact that there were things about his life—a lot of things—that he hadn't told me.

I guess I was still thinking about Cami and Kirk when I met Danny later that afternoon at the boathouse, and it put me in kind of a funny mood.

I was quiet as we climbed into a rowboat together and paddled it out onto the lake. After a few moments Danny broke the silence.

"That was kind of weird this morning at breakfast with your dad, huh?" he commented. "I mean, it was sort of a strange way to meet him."

"He only asked you for coffee like that because he didn't know who you were," I said, a little defensively. "I mean, he just thought you were someone who worked there."

Danny let out a little laugh. "Well, he was right. That is who I am."

We floated in silence for a moment.

"You know what I mean, Danny," I said softly.

"I guess . . ." He stared off at the lake. "Sometimes it's hard to be with you when it's like that, though, Jess. When I'm working. I wish we could have more times like this, when we can just be together."

"That reminds me. What about the Fourth of July party on Sunday?" I asked. "Are you working then?"

"Well, no," he answered. "I have the afternoon and the night off."

"Great!" I said. "We can go to the party together."

A pained expression crossed his face. "I'm sorry, Jess, but I can't. I have to leave here at two, right after my shift at the tennis courts."

"Why?" I asked, disappointed. "Where are you going?"

"I've got some really important business I have to take care of," he replied.

I frowned. I was getting pretty fed up with Danny's mysterious disappearing act.

"I can't believe you don't want to go with me," I said, hurt.

He put his hand on my arm. "It has nothing to do with you, believe me, Jess."

"Now you sound just like my father," I murmured to myself.

"What?"

"Oh, nothing," I muttered in frustration. "I just don't see why you have to have so many secrets."

"They're not secrets," he replied. "It's just that . . . well, there are just some things I can't talk about right now."

"Oh, big difference," I said sarcastically.

"Listen, Jess." Now he sounded angry. "I'm not the only one with secrets. You have secrets too."

"What are you talking about?" I asked.

"Me, for example," said Danny. "Admit it. You weren't in any hurry for your family to know about me. Anyone could see that."

I didn't know what to say. He was right, in a way. I looked away.

"Like I said, Jess, we're from two different worlds," Danny said quietly. "Let's just face it."

Neither of us said anything as he paddled the boat back to shore.

*Maybe he's right,* I thought miserably. *Maybe Danny and I are from two different worlds. Maybe we weren't meant to be together after all.*

# THIRTEEN

"ARE YOU SURE we should be doing this?" I asked Cami as the two of us tramped through the woods to the tennis courts early Sunday afternoon.

"Jess, you want to find out what he's up to, right?" asked Cami.

"Well, yeah," I replied, "but I just don't know if sneaking around is the way to do it."

Cami stopped. "Okay, you tried asking him about it, but he wouldn't tell you, right?"

I nodded.

"So you have no choice. You have to sneak," Cami concluded. "Shhh, look. There he is."

I peered through the bushes. Danny was there, hosing down one of the courts.

"What time is it?" Cami asked me.

I checked my watch. "Five of two. He should be finishing up soon."

"Come on," Cami whispered. "Let's go around in front of the clubhouse. He'll probably come out that way. Then we can follow him and see where he goes."

We crept quietly around the building.

"Cami, what if he sees us?" I said nervously.

"If he sees us, we say we're here to play tennis," she whispered.

When we got to the front of the building, I saw Danny's beat-up red pickup.

"That's his truck," I said, pointing.

Cami's eyes widened. "It is? That's great! Come on!" She started for the truck.

I followed her. "What are you doing?"

"Getting in," she replied.

I stared at her. "Cami, you must be joking."

"How else do you expect to follow him?" She pulled me over to the truck. In the back was a worn-looking tire, a couple of empty wooden crates, and a paint-splattered drop cloth. "Perfect," said Cami. "We can hide under this stuff." She started to climb in.

I rubbed my sweaty palms nervously on my jeans. "Wait, Cami. Stop. What if he finds us?"

"He's not going to find us, Jess," she assured me. "Just try to stop worrying, okay? This is your chance."

I hesitated.

"Come on," she urged. "He'll probably be out here any minute. Get in the truck with me now or let's forget about this."

"Okay, okay." I followed her into the back of

the pickup, my heart pounding. Together we quickly arranged the tire and the crates around us and covered ourselves with the drop cloth. My whole body was shaking.

A moment later I heard footsteps on the gravel beside the truck. I held my breath, willing my heart to stop pounding. A door in the truck's cab opened and then shut with a bang. The engine started. Cami nudged me under the drop cloth. I let out my breath in a burst.

As we bounced along the road Cami and I tried desperately to keep the crates and the drop cloth in place. I was terrified that we'd come uncovered, that Danny would see us.

A few minutes later the truck came to a stop. I heard the door open, followed by footsteps walking away. Carefully Cami and I peered out from under the drop cloth.

We were parked in front of the barracks. Danny was walking away from us, toward his room.

At the sight of him I felt a pang of guilt. What was I doing, sneaking around like this? Didn't I love Danny? Didn't I trust him?

Then I thought back to how secretive he'd been. If Danny couldn't trust me, why should I trust him?

"Hey, what is this place?" Cami asked, looking around.

"Staff housing," I explained. "They call it the barracks. I guess he stopped to get his stuff."

Sure enough, a moment later Danny reappeared, carrying a duffel bag and his guitar case. Now I was more curious than ever. And a little upset too. Danny had said he needed to take care of some "important business" today. What kind of business could he possibly need his guitar for?

Danny approached the truck. I tugged Cami's arm, and we slipped back under the drop cloth.

Suddenly something heavy landed on top of me. I tried not to gasp. Danny must have tossed his duffel bag in the back. I braced myself for the guitar to follow, but he must have decided to keep it up front with him. Shortly afterward I heard the truck door slam shut.

As the engine started again I shifted the duffel bag off my back. Cami and I struggled with the crates again as we bounced down what must have been the dirt road for another couple of minutes. Then we made a sharp turn onto a much smoother road.

"I guess he's headed toward town or something," Cami whispered.

"I just hope we get there soon," I responded. Holding everything in place back there was getting pretty tough, especially now that the truck was going faster and the wind was hitting us.

After about fifteen minutes the truck slowed down and made a turn. Shortly afterward it pulled to a stop. I willed myself to lie completely still as I heard the truck door open. My heart was pounding. I knew that if Danny caught us, I'd have no possible explanation for what we were doing back there. I'd have no choice but to admit I was following him.

I held my breath as Danny removed the duffel bag from the back of the truck.

Cami and I waited in silence until his footsteps had disappeared.

Then she nudged me. "Okay, come on; let's see where we are."

Slowly, cautiously, we lifted our heads and moved the drop cloth a little. I squinted into the sunlight.

The truck was parked in an isolated area in a small parking lot in front of a three-story, gray stone building.

Carefully Cami and I climbed out of the truck. I gazed up at the building. There were black wrought iron bars on the windows. Carved in a stone panel above the front door were the words *Beaverkill Juvenile Facility*.

"Juvenile facility; what does that mean?" Cami breathed beside me.

"It must be some kind of . . . institution," I said, still confused. *What is this place? What is Danny doing here?*

Cami's eyes widened. "You mean like a mental hospital or something?"

Suddenly my heart sank with realization. "No, Cami," I said quietly. "I think it's a detention home."

"What?" Cami stared at me.

"A reform school, a place for juvenile criminals," I said, my voice cracking a little. "Prison for kids, okay?"

"Wow," said Cami. "That is beyond intense. I wonder why Danny's here."

"Don't you see?" I cried. "He *lives* here. This is his big secret."

"Oh, no, come on, Jess," said Cami. She put her hand on my arm. "We don't know that for sure."

"Cami, it makes perfect sense," I said. "Think about it. The reason he's always disappearing from the hotel for days at a time is that he really lives here. He's probably on some kind of work program. You know, like those prisoners who they let out to clean highways and stuff."

Cami stared at me in astonishment. "You think?"

I nodded. But I almost couldn't believe it myself. Danny, a *criminal!* A hard lump formed in my throat.

"Wow," said Cami. "I wonder what he did."

I blinked back the tears. "How could he keep something like this from me?"

"Jess, I still think you might be jumping to conclusions," said Cami. "Maybe he doesn't live here. Maybe he came here for some other reason."

"Like what?" I said.

Suddenly Cami grabbed my arm. "Quick, hide! I think I see him coming back out the front door!"

I panicked. "Get in the truck!" I hissed.

"There's no time," said Cami. "Hurry! This way!"

We crouched down behind the truck and scurried from there to the nearest car—a blue station wagon. My heart was in my throat. I wished we had never decided to go through with this crazy idea. I was sure he was going to see us. We were only a few yards from Danny's truck, and there was no place to hide.

We sat there, hunched down behind the station wagon, and waited. But Danny never appeared. There was no sign of him.

"Are you sure you saw him?" I whispered to Cami.

She nodded. "Let me check again."

"Be careful," I whispered.

Slowly she raised herself up and peered over the edge of the hood of the station wagon. When she came back down, she had a funny look on her face.

"Did you see him?" I asked.

She nodded.

"What's he doing? Is he coming this way?" I asked. *Why is she acting so peculiar?*

I inched up along the side of the car to see for myself. Cami put a hand on my arm. "Jess, don't."

But it was too late. I had already spotted Danny, standing in front of the stone building. And he wasn't alone. Danny was with another girl, and he had his arm around her shoulders!

I felt sick. I sank back down to the ground. I didn't know what to do. I felt like I couldn't breathe, like someone had just punched me in the stomach.

Cami tugged on my arm. "Come on, Jess."

I closed my eyes tight. I wished I could just disappear.

"Jess," Cami said again. "Let's go."

"Where?" I managed to croak.

"Anywhere," she answered. "Out of here. Back to the hotel. Come on. We'll sneak behind those hedges over there and start down the road. It shouldn't take us too long to get back."

I followed Cami's commands as if in a dream. I felt completely numb, in shock. I was almost unable to believe what I had seen. *It can't be true. It can't.*

As Cami pulled me behind the bushes I turned for one last look at Danny. I had to be sure. I had to see again for myself.

What I saw made me feel sick. Danny and the girl were still standing together, facing each other now and talking intently. I imagined him opening his heart to her, telling her everything he wouldn't tell me. Even from this distance I could see that the girl was pretty—a little shorter than Danny, with short, reddish brown hair and sharp features. My heart felt as if it were being pulled out of my chest.

*How could I have been so stupid? How could I have trusted him?* I had believed the promises in Danny's eyes, believed that he'd be there for me. But he really loved someone else. It turned out that Danny was just like my dad, making promises he couldn't keep. I would never trust any boy again—not ever!

# FOURTEEN

"OH, COME ON, Jess, you *have* to go," Cami called to me from the bathroom off our room.

I lay curled in a ball on my bed, in the same position I'd been in since we got back to the hotel. Luckily for us, one of the hotel's waitresses on her way to work stopped and picked us up. We told her we'd started out on an early morning hike and went a little too far. If she'd noticed my bloodshot eyes, she didn't say anything.

"I really don't feel like going, Cami."

"It'll be fun," she insisted. "Dean won't be around until eight. We can check out the barbecue together."

I sighed. "I don't feel like eating." I didn't feel like doing much of anything—except crying. Ever since I'd seen Danny with that girl I'd felt devastated, like the world had crumbled around me.

Cami came out of the bathroom. She was wearing her red Chinese silk robe, and she had her hair wrapped in a towel. She looked at me seriously. "Jessica Graham, I hope you realize that today is our nation's birthday. It's your civic responsibility to gorge on barbecued chicken and watch fireworks."

I smiled a little in spite of how rotten I was feeling. "Since when did you get so patriotic?"

"Probably ever since I came up with this idea." She unwrapped the towel from her head.

I sat up and let out a little gasp. Cami's ringlets were streaked with red and blue stripes.

She grinned. "Like it?"

"It's wild," I told her. "Will it wash out?"

She shrugged. "I hope so. Wait till you see the rest of my outfit." She smiled. "It's a real tribute to our nation. And it's definitely going to set off some fireworks with Dean."

I laughed. "I bet."

Cami sat down on the bed with me. "Come on, Jess. Go to the party with me. Just for a little while. You can't stay in here and cry for the rest of the summer." She put her arm around my shoulders. "You can't waste your whole summer feeling down about a guy who would do something like that."

I felt my eyes well up again. "Cami, how could he do that to me?"

Cami sighed. "Easy, Jess. Because on some level, all guys are the exact same thing—pond scum."

★　　　★　　　★

135

The hotel had set up a big white tent on one of the lawns, with tables and chairs inside and several huge barbecues nearby. Even though eating was the last thing I felt like doing right then, I followed Cami through the buffet line and loaded my plate up with chicken, corn on the cob, potato salad, and a bunch of other stuff.

As Cami and I looked for seats we realized we'd forgotten to take plastic silverware and napkins.

"I'll go back and get it," I volunteered.

"Okay, I'll get us a table," Cami said. "Here, give me your plate."

As I approached the buffet area again a gray-haired man in a white cook's cap who was turning hot dogs on a grill caught my eye and smiled.

Almost automatically I smiled back.

"You're Jess, aren't you?" the man said.

"Yes," I said, surprised. "How did you know my name?"

"I'm Sam," the man explained. "I work with young Danny."

"Oh," I said, feeling sadness and disappointment flood through me again at the mention of Danny's name.

"That young fella sure seems to have taken a shine to you," Sam said. "You must be a very special girl."

*Apparently not special enough,* I said silently. I felt tears forming at the back of my eyes and turned my head.

"I better go," I mumbled. "Nice to meet you."

I grabbed the silverware and hurriedly turned

away. As I did I almost smacked right into my father, who was standing with Janie. They both had plates of food in their hands.

"Whoa, watch out there, Jess," he said good-naturedly.

"Oh, sorry, Dad," I said in a low voice, still blinking back tears. I tried not to meet his eye.

"Are you all right?" Janie asked. "You look a little upset."

"I'm fine," I lied. I forced a little laugh. "I think I just got some smoke from the barbecue in my eyes."

"Well, let's all go find a seat," said my father. "Where's Cami?"

"She's already sitting," I said. I pointed. "Right over there."

"Fine, fine," said my father. "Let's go join her."

We walked over to where Cami was sitting. Amazingly, Janie didn't even seem to notice Cami's red-and-blue hair or her outfit—a tiny red-and-white-striped baby tee with blue boxer shorts rolled down at the waist to reveal a star she'd painted around her belly button with red lipstick. I supposed Janie was finally getting used to Cami.

After I'd picked at my food for a while, Cami shot me a look and pointed quickly to her wrist. I glanced at my watch and then turned my arm so she could see it. It was almost eight o'clock.

Cami yawned and stretched elaborately. "Mmmm, that was good. Boy, am I full. Want to take a little walk with me, Jess?"

I knew what she was looking for—a way to get away from the table so she could go meet Dean in the parking lot. "Yeah, sure," I said.

We stood up.

"Don't wander off too far," my father advised. "The fireworks start at nine."

When we were out of earshot of my father and Janie, Cami turned to me. "Are you okay, Jess? You seemed pretty down during dinner."

"I am down," I admitted. I bit my lip. "Cami, I know I should forget about him, but I can't."

"Why don't you come watch the fireworks with me and Dean?" Cami offered.

I managed a smile. I knew she was just trying to be nice. "That's okay."

"No, really, Jess," she urged. "You should."

"Thanks, Cami," I said. "Maybe I'll see you down there in a little while." I looked at my watch. "It's after eight. You better go."

She wrinkled her forehead with concern. "Are you sure you're okay?"

I nodded. "Go."

"Okay, catch you later at the lake."

I watched her hurry away. Why was it that things always seemed to come so easily to Cami? She hopped from guy to guy like it was nothing, like a little kid going through a bag of Halloween candy. Why couldn't I be more like her? It was obviously a big mistake to have let myself care so much about one guy. I could see that now.

But it was almost as though I hadn't had any choice—not once I had looked into Danny's eyes.

A voice cut into my thoughts. "Excuse me?"

I turned. It was Quentin, the guy who'd given us the ride that day from the mall.

"Oh, hi," I said.

"Hi," he answered. He rubbed his hands on his jeans. He looked nervous. "Um, I was just wondering if I could talk to you about something."

"Okay, sure." I didn't exactly feel like talking, but he seemed so eager and so agitated.

His face colored. "This is kind of hard for me to do, but, um, I kind of wanted to ask you about your friend Cami."

I wasn't exactly surprised. I waited.

"It's just that, well, I . . . does she have a boyfriend?" he blurted finally.

I sighed. Suddenly I just couldn't take it anymore.

"Only about a hundred!" I burst out. The tears came back to my eyes. "Only just about any guy in the world she wants, that's all!"

Quentin was staring at me, but I didn't care. I felt a sob escape me. It just wasn't fair. Every guy in the universe was interested in Cami, but I couldn't even have one—the only one I cared about! I turned and ran away.

At first I was just running, not even knowing where I was going, just trying to get away from everyone and everything. Finally I headed for the woods, the trails. I ran, sobbing, stumbling over the rocks and dirt, tree limbs scratching at my face. I just wanted to get away from everyone.

After a few minutes I collapsed at the base of a tree, exhausted. I wiped the tears away from my face, still breathing heavily, and looked around. I was on a trail, but I wasn't sure which one. I stood up and started to walk.

The trail emerged from the woods, and I realized with a start where I was. In front of me were the barracks—and parked right outside them was Danny's truck!

I was surprised and suddenly very angry. Danny was back, and I wanted to confront him, to tell him that I knew all about him, the way he'd lied to me. I walked determinedly toward building number five.

But when I got there, I stopped in my tracks. Danny's window was illuminated, and I could see inside his room. He was there, standing, leaning against the wall and talking to someone.

I moved closer, creeping quietly through the grass. I climbed up onto a tree stump and peered inside the room. There, sitting on the bed opposite Danny, was the girl I'd seen him with that afternoon!

I couldn't believe my eyes. *Cami's right,* I thought furiously, *all boys are pond scum—and Danny is the scummiest of them all!*

On the other side of the woods the fireworks started over the lake. I stood there in the dark, unable to move. Each distant explosion felt like a bullet in my heart.

# FIFTEEN

THE FOLLOWING MORNING I put on my nicest sundress and borrowed some plum lipstick from Cami. I brushed my hair and left it down.

The truth was, I wasn't exactly looking forward to seeing Danny at breakfast, but I knew I couldn't hide from him for the rest of our time there. So I was going to do the next-best thing. I was going to look so good that he'd have to see how stupid he'd been to mess up his chances with me.

Unfortunately my eyes were still a little puffy from crying, so I borrowed a pair of Cami's sunglasses.

I spotted Danny the minute we walked into the dining room. He was carrying a mop and bucket across the room to clean up a spill. He glanced my way, but I turned my head quickly, pretending to be deep in conversation with Cami.

"Hey, isn't that your young man over there?" asked my father. "Maybe we should ask to sit in the area where he's working today."

"No, Dad, no!" I said quickly. "I mean, that's over. He's not my 'young man.' Not anymore."

Janie looked at me in surprise. "Is it over between you two, dear? So soon?"

"Gee, I never even got to know him," said my father.

"Believe me, you didn't miss a thing," I muttered.

As we followed the hostess to our seats Danny glanced up and noticed me. He smiled at me. I turned away quickly. I sighed. This wasn't going to be easy.

But somehow I made it through breakfast without catching his eye once. Every time I sensed him looking at me, I would turn to talk to Cami or act like I was busy with my food.

Finally it was over. As the four of us turned to leave the dining room Cami turned to me.

"Nicely done, Jess," she whispered.

"I can't believe I have to spend the rest of the vacation here, seeing him," I whispered back miserably.

"Girls, what do you say to another game of doubles this morning?" asked my father, cutting in. "Maybe I can get us a court."

"No, Dad," I said without hesitation. The last thing I wanted in the mood I was in was to play tennis with my dad and Janie. "I'm tired," I added. "I just want to lie by the pool or something."

"Sounds good to me," Cami said.

"Boy, I thought young people were supposed to have energy," my father commented. He grinned. "What you two need to do is spend a summer on a farm. Build up your stamina."

Both Cami and I groaned.

My father laughed. "We'll talk about it. Maybe next year."

A little while later Cami and I lay on a couple of lounges by the pool in our bathing suits. I could feel sad thoughts of Danny starting to invade my brain, so I picked up my book to try to tune them out. I was almost at the end of *Grandma's Little Angels.*

Cami lay beside me, her face turned toward the sun. "Hey, Jess, I almost forgot," she said after a few minutes. "What are you doing tonight?"

I put my book down on my lap. "Oh, I have tons of plans," I said sarcastically. "Seventeen dates, fifty parties, a formal ball—lots of stuff. What do you *think* I'm doing?"

She laughed. "Want to go to a rave?"

I sat up, interested. I'd never actually been to a rave before. I'd seen some stuff about them in magazines, and this girl in my Spanish class at school had told me about one she'd been to near the Everglades, about an hour or so from South Beach.

"Where?" I asked.

"Some farm near here," Cami responded. "Dean told me about it last night. They've had a few raves this summer. They're supposed to be fun. He said he'd give us a ride."

"I don't know," I said. "What am I going to tell my father?"

Cami laughed. "Well, he did say you should spend some time on a farm, didn't he?"

I rolled my eyes. "I hardly think that this is the kind of farm experience he meant."

Cami shrugged. "Then lie. Tell him we're going to play Ping-Pong or something." She twisted to look at me. "You should go, Jess. You need to have some fun. It'll help take your mind off—*Danny!*" She gaped at a spot above my head.

I turned around. Danny was standing behind me, his head cocked and his eyes trained on mine accusingly. A stack of fresh towels was in his hands.

"Towel, miss?" he said in a slightly sarcastic tone.

"No, thank you," I said coolly. I picked up my book and started to read. Correction: I pretended to read, I *tried* to read, but I was really just staring at the words on the page in front of me.

Danny was still standing behind me.

"Jess," he said, his whisper an angry hiss. "What is going on? Why are you acting so strange?"

I tossed my head. "I'm definitely not the one who's been acting strange, Danny. You are."

"I don't know what you're talking about," he protested. "You were the one who wouldn't even look at me all through breakfast."

"Um, maybe I should go," Cami said.

"No, stay here, Cami," I said. I glanced at Danny and then turned my back toward him. "Let's talk more about tonight, about the rave. This sounds like so much fun." I did my best to make my voice sound enthusiastic.

"Jess," Danny pleaded.

I ignored him.

*"Jess,"* he said again.

I turned to him angrily. "Excuse me, but I'm trying to talk to my friend right now." I glared at him. "Don't you have some towels to hand out or something?"

He stared at me, his eyes full of hurt and confusion. For a moment I almost felt sorry for him. But then I remembered—the reform school, the girl in his room, the lies. I turned back to my book.

"I knew it," Danny said angrily. His voice was shaking. "You're just a snobby rich girl after all. I knew what you were like in the beginning."

I stood up, furious. *How dare he call me names after what he's done to me?*

"Yeah, well, I wish I'd known what you were like in the beginning, Danny Jordan!" I screamed. Everyone at the pool was looking at us, but I didn't care. "If I had, I definitely would have stayed as far away from you as possible!"

Before I even knew what I was doing, I lunged for his stack of towels and threw them in the pool.

There was an awful silence. Everyone was looking at me—Cami, Danny, the old people with visors on their heads and white stuff on their noses—even the two little girls who had been splashing in the shallow end of the pool. The towels were slowly sinking to the bottom.

Without another word I turned and ran. As fast as I could I charged up the path toward the bungalow.

I had to get out of there, I knew that. I couldn't stay at the pool another moment or at Golden's either. Not as long as Danny was working there. I had to find my dad. I wanted to go home right away—and never, ever see Danny Jordan's face again.

# SIXTEEN

"**B**UT DAD, YOU have to let me," I pleaded. "I can't stay here anymore."

"Jessica, you haven't even told me what's wrong," my father objected.

"Is it that boy, Danny?" asked Janie. "Is that what's bothering you, Jess?"

"I don't want to talk about it," I said stubbornly. *And especially not with you,* I added silently.

"I'm sorry, Jess, but you know I can't send you home," said my father. "Your mother is still in Pensacola, and I promised to take care of you until she gets home."

"Then let's go to your place in New York," I said, desperate. "We can stay there for the rest of the time. Anyplace but here."

My father scratched his chin. "Well, I suppose that might be a consideration. I hadn't thought of that."

"Peter, you can't be serious," Janie cried.

"Well, it would give you a chance to get some more work done on the Klein case," my father said.

"I'm doing plenty of work on that case up here," Janie responded. "Whatever needs to be done in New York can be handled by Kevin and the other paralegals. Peter, this is our vacation! We can't cut it short just because, because . . ."

"Because *I* want to," I finished angrily. I turned to my father. "You never do anything I ask you, never! I didn't want to come here in the first place, but you and Mom made me. No one ever listens to what I want."

"Jess, dear, whatever this little problem of yours is, I'm sure it won't seem nearly as important in a few days," Janie said carefully.

*I hate you,* I said silently. *Why do you always have to talk to me like I'm a kindergartner?*

"Janie's right," said my father. "Why don't you give yourself some time? I'm sure things will work out."

"Thanks a lot!" I shot out. "Thanks for nothing!" I turned and stormed out the door.

Unfortunately it was the *front* door I stormed out of instead of the door to my room, so I found myself standing alone outside in the woods. I have to admit, I felt kind of silly.

I walked around the back of the bungalow and opened the door to my own room. Cami was waiting there for me on her bed.

"Another great performance from Jessica

147

Graham," she joked. "And this one was a double feature. I have to say, though, I preferred the first half, by the pool. The towels were a great touch. The walking around the bungalow part in this one confused me a little, though."

I laughed a little, in spite of how I was feeling. "I was trying to get my dad to send me home," I explained.

"I know," she responded. "Actually, I think most of Galaxy Circle knows too. No luck, huh?"

I shook my head. "Cami, I just don't know how I'm going to stand it, seeing Danny around here for the rest of our stay. I wish he would just quit or something."

Cami raised an eyebrow meaningfully. "Who knows? Maybe he'll get fired."

"What do you mean?" I asked.

"Oh, I don't know," she said. "It could probably be arranged. No one's a perfect employee, right? All we'd have to do is make sure the management found out about any little thing Danny happened to be doing wrong."

For a moment I felt a pang. Did I really want to get Danny fired? Wasn't that a little drastic? Then I thought again about what he had done, about the way I'd felt seeing him with that girl. The more I thought about it, the better Cami's idea began to sound.

"But how would we do it?" I asked.

"Well, for starters, there's that girl you saw in his room," Cami said. "I wonder how Golden's management would feel if they knew about that?"

"That's right!" I cried. "Danny told me that staff members aren't allowed to have guests in their rooms." *Especially guests who might be criminals.*

Cami got an evil glint in her eye. "So all we have to do is let somebody at the hotel know what Danny's been up to so they can be on the lookout. He's bound to take her there again, right? And next time he does, they'll catch him in the act."

"But who will we tell?" I asked. "And how?"

Cami smiled. "You leave that up to me. I'll just head over to the management office and get friendly with someone. When the time is right, I'll let it drop that one of the employees has been inviting girls to his room. Danny Jordan will be history."

I knew I should be pleased about what Cami had said. I knew I should feel really happy that we'd figured out a way to get Danny away from Golden's for good. After all, he'd lied to me and been unfaithful and hurt me worse than I'd ever been hurt in my life. I should be thrilled that we were getting rid of him.

So why did I feel so sad?

# SEVENTEEN

THAT NIGHT CAMI and I stood on the highway near the turnoff for Golden's, waiting for Dean to pick us up for the rave.

"Are you sure he's coming?" I asked Cami as she peered down the dark road.

"I hope so," she replied. "I get the feeling he's not the most reliable person in the world, though. It was almost nine when he finally showed up to meet me last night. I thought we were going to miss the fireworks." She laughed a little. "Turned out we didn't see that much of them anyway. We were kind of busy."

I was silent, thinking of where I'd been the night before when the fireworks started, standing on the tree stump outside Danny's window. Then I remembered the cruise to the Bahamas I was supposed to have been on with Jeremy. This had definitely turned out to be the worst Fourth of July of my whole life.

"Oh, by the way," Cami said. "Mission accomplished on that little 'employee problem' we were talking about earlier."

I turned to her. "You mean Danny? What did you do?" I had a funny feeling in my stomach all of a sudden.

"Let's just say I dropped some important information with the right people over at the management office," Cami said slyly.

I wanted to ask her more, but at that moment a car pulled up in front of us. Inside the beat-up Camaro with the patched paint job were Dean and two other guys. One of them had a thin face and long, stringy blond hair. The other one, who was sitting in the back, had a buzz cut. All three of them grinned at us.

I glanced at Cami. "Who are those other guys?" I whispered.

"I don't know. Friends of Dean's, I guess." She pulled open the front door. "Hi, Dean."

The blond guy got out and grinned at me. I noticed he had a chipped tooth. "Hey, I'm Cal."

I tried to smile politely. "Hi."

The guy in the back flipped the front passenger seat forward. "One of you can ride back here with me," he offered.

"That's okay," said Cami. "Jess and I will ride up front together."

Cal shrugged and climbed in the back. Cami slid in the front next to Dean, and I climbed in after her. As soon as I pulled the door shut Dean raced off down the road. He popped a tape in the deck, and loud guitar music started to wail.

"My cousin's tape!" Dean yelled over the din. "I'm going to try to get the DJ to play it tonight."

Cal leaned over the front seat and passed me a quart bottle of beer with about three sips left in it.

"Uh, no, but thanks anyway," I said, eyeing the frothy swill at the bottom.

"Pass it this way!" Dean called. He stuck out his hand.

Reluctantly I gave him the bottle. There wasn't much in there, certainly not enough to affect him, but I got the feeling it wasn't the first drink he'd had that night.

"Hey, Dean, why don't you ease up," Cami said. "You're driving."

"Ah, we're almost there anyway," he replied. "Open up another one of those brewskies, Ray."

There was a hiss as a bottle was opened. The buzz cut guy handed it over the seat to Dean, who took a long, hard swallow. I eyed Cami. I was starting to wonder if I'd made the right decision. This did not look too promising. Cami raised her eyebrows and shrugged.

Luckily a few moments later we pulled off the road to a large, dirt-covered area where a bunch of other cars were already parked. When Dean stopped the car, I could hear music in the distance. We all headed in the direction of the music.

Cal snickered behind me as we tramped through a field of tall grass.

"If old man Gunther could only see us now," he said.

"Gunther, who's that?" asked Cami.

"The guy whose farm this is," Dean said. "Or used to be. He died last spring."

"Then whose place is it now?" I wondered out loud.

"Nobody's really," Dean said. "Well, Gunther's got a nephew who owns it now, but he's from the city, so he's not working the place." He laughed. "Makes it the perfect spot for a party like this."

"Yeah, as long as the cops don't hassle us," added Ray.

"You mean we're not supposed to be here?" I asked, a little nervously.

"Course not." Ray snorted. "That's what it's all about. It's like a pirate thing."

Cal put his arm around my shoulders. "Don't worry, I'll protect you if the cops come."

I gently shrugged him off and took a couple of large strides to put distance between us. "Uh, thanks."

"I'm sure it'll be okay, Jess," Cami said.

I hoped so. The last thing I wanted was trouble with the police. Somehow I didn't think my dad would take it too well.

Finally we arrived at a fenced-in corral full of people. It was really crowded—it looked like there were a couple hundred people there—and everyone was dancing. Looking around, I was totally amazed that a party this big and elaborate had actually been set up on someone's land without anyone's permission. The DJ sat high on a wooden platform above the crowd at one end of the corral. Music blared from speakers elevated on metal poles around the perimeter, and purple beams of light projected from above the DJ's stand skimmed the crowd.

A series of slides was being projected against the wall of a large barn nearby. At first the pictures were hard to make out; they just seemed to be abstract collections of blobs and lines. After a few moments, though, I realized that they were blown up microscopic images—cells and amoebas and stuff.

Dean climbed over the fence into the corral full of people and then helped Cami over the fence. Cal grinned at me.

"That's okay," I said, reading his mind. "I can do it okay on my own." I pulled myself up over the fence and came down on the other side at the edge of the huge crowd.

Everyone around me was dancing, jumping up and down in unison. Cami was bouncing alongside me, her eyes shining.

"Isn't this great?" she yelled. She grabbed my hand. "Come on!"

I followed her deeper into the crowd. This was like nothing I had ever experienced before. There were people everywhere I looked, tightly packed, dancing together as one. It was like being in a tremendous ocean of people. Almost involuntarily I started dancing too, matching my rhythm to the pulsing movements of the crowd around me.

A purple laser beam skimmed the top of the crowd. As it passed by, all the dancers around me raised their arms in the air, creating a froth of purple-tinted hands. As the beam of light traveled over the crowd hands went up to meet it, disappearing again when the light moved on. The light came back, and I threw my hands in the air too. I could see Cami dancing a couple of people away from me, with Dean not too far away. Cal and Ray were nowhere in sight.

Cami smiled at me, a great, huge beaming smile. I smiled back. This was fun.

Now the dancers closest to me were changing their rhythm, stamping their feet and rolling their heads from side to side. As if by magic, the music changed too. Suddenly everyone was stamping their feet and rolling their heads from side to side.

I stamped and rolled. The rolling was making me dizzy, but I loved the way it felt. This felt good. It felt free. Suddenly nothing mattered—not Danny, not my dad and Janie, not anything. I laughed out loud. A girl dancing next to me laughed too. Then someone else laughed, and someone else, and someone else. Soon everyone was laughing around me. The corral became one huge laughing organism, a great laugh released up into the night sky.

I felt amazing, like I was part of something huge. I rolled my head. I was sweating. The world was spinning.

I paused a moment to look for Cami. She was nowhere in sight. The crowd had swallowed her up. I spotted Cal dancing a little ways away. I danced through the crowd to reach him.

"Have you seen Cami?" I screamed above the din.

He grinned at me and pointed to his ears to show he hadn't heard me.

I stood up on my tiptoes to get closer to his face. He bent down toward me. His breath smelled like beer.

I yelled in his face. "I'm looking for—"

He cut me off by putting his mouth on mine. I pulled back in shock and disgust. His kiss had been wet and beery.

He grinned at me again. I turned away from him and pushed my way through the crowd as fast as I could. I wiped at my mouth.

*Where is Cami?* I scanned the crowd. It seemed there were even more people in the corral now; things were getting very tight. Dancing, swaying bodies bumped me on all sides. I was sweaty and thirsty. I searched for a path, a way out. Maybe if I could get to the edge of the crowd, I could climb up on the fence and look for Cami.

It was no use. I was lost. I couldn't get my bearings, couldn't see above the people to locate the fence. The moving sea of dancers seemed to go on forever, seemed to be closing in on me. I felt penned in, panicky. I pushed my way through the crowd again. But everywhere I looked, there were more people.

"Cami!" I cried. But my voice was no match for the pulse of the music, the happy roar of the crowd.

I stumbled into a part of the crowd where people were whirling around, their faces upturned and their arms outstretched. I ducked flying limbs, trying to get someplace, anyplace. It was like making my way through the gears inside a clock or a car wash. I dodged arms, hands. I put my hands up to protect my face. I couldn't see where I was going.

Somebody in the distance screamed. The scream grew and magnified. I couldn't tell if it was a scream of joy or pain. Then people around me began to push. The music stopped suddenly, and everyone was running. It was a stampede.

I struggled to get my balance, to get out of the way, but I tripped and fell. The ground was dark and muddy. I tried to get up, but the world was closing in on me, and my feet kept slipping. I felt like I couldn't breathe, like I had no air. I felt a million feet trample me.

I fought my way to the surface again, feeling like I was drowning. A searing pain went through my ankle.

I knew I had to get out of there or I would be crushed to death. I could hear sirens now. The police! I panicked. My father would be furious if I got arrested! *Where is Cami?*

The crowd thinned a bit as people jumped the fence. I limped off to one side. Everyone was running, and the squad cars were driving across the field toward the corral. I was penned in. I knew I'd never scale the fence with my hurt ankle. I was done for.

Suddenly someone called my name. I turned around.

It was Danny! He was standing a few yards away from me. I froze, unable to believe my own eyes. *What is he doing here?*

# EIGHTEEN

"JESS!" DANNY CALLED again. He started toward me.

I stumbled toward him and fell, yelping in pain.

Danny rushed to my side and in one quick movement scooped me up into his arms. I buried my head in his neck.

Danny walked quickly, carrying me through the crowd toward the fence.

"Don't worry, Jess, I'll get you out of here," he promised.

"Wait, I can't," I said. "Not without Cami. She's back there some—"

"Cami's fine," he cut me off. "I saw her. She was getting a ride back. She said she looked for you all over."

We were at the fence now. Quickly but carefully Danny hoisted me over, setting me down gently on the other side. He hopped over himself and lifted me up again.

"My truck's over here," he said. He carried me through an isolated area of woods to a small clearing. Danny's red truck was the only car parked there. "The police won't come this way," Danny assured me. "Everyone else is parked over on the other side of the farm." He placed me down gently on the hood of the truck.

"Danny, I'm worried," I said. "I hope Cami's not riding back with the guys who drove us here. They were drinking a lot."

"She's fine," he told me. "She's with this guy from Golden's."

"You mean Kirk?" I said in surprise.

He shook his head. "Quentin. He's a groundskeeper. His older sister's giving them both a ride." He opened the truck door and helped me inside.

Danny climbed in behind the wheel and started the truck. We drove for a while in silence.

"Is your ankle okay?" Danny asked. "I mean, should I take you to a hospital or something?"

"No, that's all right," I replied. "It's sore, but I don't think it's broken or anything."

We were silent again.

"Thanks for getting me out of there," I said finally.

He nodded. "When Cami said she lost you, I figured I'd better keep looking." He paused. "Jess, what were you doing at that thing anyway?"

"The same thing you were," I replied, a little irritated. "Having fun."

"I was there to look for someone," said Danny.

"Who?" I demanded angrily. "Your girlfriend?"

He turned to me. "Yes. At least, I thought that's who you were. Now I'm not so sure."

I stared at him in astonishment. "You went to the rave to look for *me?*"

"That's right," he said. "There have been a bunch of those things around here lately, and the police always end up breaking them up. It can be dangerous. People get hurt, arrested." He paused. "After I heard you and Cami talking about it today at the pool, I got worried. I mean, even though you treated me like you did, I still didn't want anything to happen to you," he added in a low voice.

I didn't know what to say. *Is this the truth or just another line?* I started to cry.

Danny pulled over to the side of the road. "Jessie, what is it? What's the matter?"

Now I was sobbing. *How could he make me spell it out like this?* "I saw you, Danny!" I cried. "I saw you! I know all about it!"

"All about what?" he said. "What are you talking about?"

"I was there," I said miserably. "Yesterday at the juvenile place."

His face got serious. "Okay, so you know."

"That's right!" I cried. "I know! I saw you with that girl in the afternoon, and I saw her again last night in your room." I choked on a sob. "I know you're seeing someone else."

Danny let out a laugh. I glared at him through my tears. *How can he be so cruel, so heartless?*

"I'm sorry, I'm sorry," he said quickly. He put his hand on my arm. "It's just that girl was my sister!"

I stared at him in amazement. "Your *sister?*"

"Yes," he said. "Jess, that was Lisa."

I didn't know what to say. "Danny, your sister's in reform school?" I blurted.

He shook his head and laughed again. "No, no. It's not a reform school, it's a *home.*" Now his face got serious. "You know, for kids who don't have anyone. An orphanage."

My eyes widened. "An orphanage? Your sister lives in an orphanage?"

"That's right," he said. "I do too. Or rather, I did. I'm on a work-release program so I can work at Golden's for the summer."

"So that's where you've been going?" I asked.

He nodded.

"But Danny, why didn't you tell me?"

He sighed. "I wanted to, but I didn't think you'd understand. Your family is so . . . *normal.*"

Now it was my turn to laugh. "Oh, sure. It's totally normal for your dad to leave your mom for someone he works with."

"Okay, right, your parents are divorced and stuff, but so are a lot of kids'," Danny said. "My family's . . . different. We've been through a lot of hard times."

"Everybody's family has troubles, Danny," I said softly.

"I guess," he said. He stared out the window for a moment. "After my mom died, everything fell apart.

162

My dad tried to keep the family together, but it was too much for him. He had a bunch of bad luck, lost a couple of jobs, got in some trouble." He paused. "That's when they came to take us kids away."

"How awful," I said. I realized that Danny was right; his family's troubles were a lot worse than mine. At least I'd always had my home.

"Scott and Lila went to foster homes pretty quick," Danny explained. "They were still young and cute. But Lisa and I were older, thirteen and fourteen already. Nobody wanted us. So we went to live at Beaverkill Juvenile Facility."

Something in his voice gave me a chill. "That's the place I saw you," I said. "What was it like, living there?"

Danny's face grew hard. "I hated it. I would have run away the first day if it weren't for Lisa. Instead I just started counting down. I knew when I turned eighteen, I'd be free, and I planned to take Lisa with me, try to get the whole family back together. Maybe even find my dad. Everything was going great. I had some money saved and everything. And then it all fell apart."

"What do you mean?" I asked. "What happened?"

Danny took a deep breath. I could see that this was hard for him.

"This guy who works at the home," he said finally. "One of the supervisors. His name is Mr. Lythcott. He started . . . bothering my sister."

"Bothering?" I felt my throat tighten.

Danny ran his hand through his hair. He turned to face me. "At first it was just talk. You know, comments about the way she looked and stuff. I told her to stick it out, not to make any trouble, that we'd be out of there soon. But lately things have gotten worse. That's why I've been over there so much lately."

"Oh, my gosh, Danny," I gasped. "Why didn't you report him?"

"Believe me, I wanted to kill him," Danny said, his voice hard with anger. "But this guy Lythcott's got power. It would be his word against ours. He'd have every lawyer in the world on his side. I knew no one would believe us. Besides, that would have taken too long. By the time we got anyone from the outside to check it out, it might have been too late for Lisa. I knew I had to get her out of there right away."

"So what did you do?" I asked.

"I brought her to my room at the barracks," he said. "She can't stay there long, though. Beaverkill won't notice she's gone till morning. But once they report her missing, the police will be over there to check my place in a hurry. I figure she's safe for tonight, though."

Suddenly I had an awful feeling in my stomach. "You left Lisa in your room in the barracks when you came to the rave tonight?" I asked uneasily. *What were Cami's words, that she'd "dropped some important information with the right people at the management office"?*

Danny nodded. He took my chin in his hands.

"I had to take the risk. Even after you railed into me like that at the pool, I knew I'd never forgive myself if I let anything bad happen to you." He moved toward me.

I put my hand on his arm. "Danny, stop. I want to kiss you more than anything in the world right now, believe me. But we've got to get to the barracks right away." I took a deep breath. "I think Lisa may be in trouble. And if she is, it's all my fault."

# NINETEEN

SURE ENOUGH, WHEN Danny and I pulled up in front of the barracks, two state trooper cars were parked outside. The moment the cops saw Danny's red truck, they stopped it.

"Danny Jordan?" asked one of the uniformed men.

"Yes, that's me," Danny answered in a tight voice.

"Please step out of the truck." We both climbed out, and the trooper shined his light on my face. "Who are you, miss?"

I shielded my eyes from the beam. "I'm Jessica Graham. I'm staying here at the hotel."

"You're free to go, miss," the trooper informed me. "Young man, we'd like to talk to you a bit. You can ride in the back with your sister while we drive you back to the facility."

"No!" Danny exploded. "You're not taking her back there!"

"Now, now, calm down there, Danny," said the

trooper. "You know Beaverkill is her legal residence as long as she's a minor without a guardian."

"You can't do this!" Danny cried.

I put my hand on his arm. "Danny, wait. You're not going to get anywhere with this unless you have a lawyer. I'll run get my dad."

He turned to me with hope in his eyes. "Really? Can your father help us? Does he take care of stuff like this?"

I took a deep breath. "No. But he knows someone who does. And he says she's good too. I think she might be willing to help us."

From that moment on it felt as if someone pressed the fast-forward button on our summer vacation. The next several weeks were a whirlwind of activity, with Janie taking center stage. She put everything else on hold to work on Danny's case full-time. For the first time since we'd been there, something that was important to me got priority. Correction: *top* priority. Janie got straight to business immediately, sitting us all down and explaining what she was going to do.

"There are three main goals," Janie detailed. "The first is to get Lisa removed from the juvenile facility immediately."

"How are you going to do that?" Danny had asked anxiously.

"I'm already doing it," Janie replied smoothly. "I've had my paralegals in New York draw up a temporary order to get her placed in a private home."

I could see the worry creeping into Danny's eyes

as he ventured, "I, um, really appreciate what you're doing, but what kind of private home? How do I know she'll be okay?"

I was sure Janie was about to get defensive since she didn't like being second-guessed, but I was wrong. Instead Janie put Danny's fears to rest. "Don't worry, I'm getting her into a home with a woman I know. A woman who takes in teenagers and provides them with a safe, loving home. Besides, you'll be able to call her, visit her, anything you want. It's not like Lisa's going to be a prisoner. And if for some reason Lisa's not happy there, out she comes."

Relief flooded Danny's eyes as Janie continued, "The next order of business is conducting a search for your father, Danny. Finding him is our best hope for getting your whole family back together, including your younger brother and sister, Lila and Scott."

"I've tried that myself," Danny offered wistfully, "but my dad seems to have disappeared off the face of the earth."

"Leave it to me. My law firm has all sorts of resources, including a search program on the Internet. As soon as you give me all the pertinent information about him and the younger kids, I'll get my staff right on it."

"That would be incredible, Mrs. . . . I mean, Ms. Baxter. I really appreciate it. Thank you."

Janie didn't bother with "You're welcome" but went straight to her third goal, which was, as she put it, "nailing that creep Lythcott. He's got to be held accountable and put away so no one else will ever be hurt by him. Preparing a case against him is going to take time, and it's going to have to be done here in this district. Which means I'll have to stay several more weeks, possibly until the end of the summer."

My dad jumped in. "Janie and I have already discussed this. I won't be able to stay beyond our original four weeks, so I'll be heading back to work in New York City. Janie's going to stay up here, and you girls— well, you've got a choice. You can either go back to Florida as we originally planned, or you can stay here with Janie. Providing, Jess, it's okay with your mother, and Cami, if it's okay with your parents."

Before my dad had even finished, I'd made my decision. By the expression on Cami's face I knew she'd made hers too. Convincing our respective parents would be a snap.

As Janie got up, signaling the end of this meeting, she turned to Danny and said sincerely, "You know, it was really courageous of you to try to take all this on by yourself, Danny. You're quite a special young man."

Danny's cheeks reddened.

So did mine when my dad added, "Of course he is. My daughter has excellent taste in men. Just like you do, Janie." Then it was her turn to blush.

My dad patted Danny on the shoulder. "By the way, about your job. It was a stroke of bad luck that the hotel found out about Lisa being in your room—"

Cami and I looked at each other, feeling sick for what we had done.

"But you can rest assured that you're being fully reinstated."

"I am?" Danny asked hopefully.

"Leave it to my future wife." Dad beamed proudly.

And that's exactly what we did. We left it all in Janie's hands. Very capable hands, I had to admit. The whole time we'd been here, Janie had acted like such a nitpicking stickler for perfection, which had annoyed Cami and me to no end. Only now it seemed like that trait was Janie's best quality.

By the next day she had, as promised, gotten Lisa placed in a safe home. Danny and my dad had taken her there. When they returned, Danny told me, "I think this is going to work out really well. There are other kids there Lisa's age, and she and her roommate have already bonded."

Janie had also filed papers for the case against Lythcott and had her office working on finding Danny's father, brother, and other sister.

A couple of days later my dad had to go back to work. We stayed on in the Mercury bungalow, only Cami and I switched rooms with Janie. "The back room is quieter," she'd said. "I'll get more done there."

Cami and I got more done too—getting to know our new boyfriends—when they weren't working, that is. Danny resumed his four jobs at Golden's. Even though he wasn't desperate anymore, trying to stockpile enough money so he could spring Lisa from the facility, he explained, "I made the commitment to handle all four jobs for the whole summer, and I'm going to fulfill it." Danny was so honorable. It made me love him even more.

Meanwhile Cami's cutie, Quentin, went about his gardening duties with new energy and a permanent smile pasted to his face. In fact, Cami and Quentin actually stayed a couple for the rest of the summer, which meant that in an odd way, Cami actually got her wish—to go out with someone really different!

Whenever Danny finished work for the day, we were together. It felt like a never-ending dream, my best one ever. We went swimming in the pool, boating on the lake. When my sprained ankle healed, we even played tennis doubles with Cami and Quentin. Correction: Cami and I played tennis—we taught the boys the basics, only neither one was very good.

One day Danny and I went horseback riding and took along a picnic lunch that Danny had prepared from the hotel's kitchen. He'd snagged a blanket from the staff linen closet, and when we came to a clearing off the trail in the woods, he spread it out and we shared sandwiches, sodas, and a huge slice of chocolate cake. Danny told me more about his childhood and how close all four kids had been before tragedy struck. He told me about his mom, Lena, and how brave she had been through her illness. And he told me how he used to blame his father for letting the family fall apart.

"I can't tell you how many nights I lay in bed, wide awake, hating him," Danny divulged. "I don't know if you can understand what that feels like, Jess."

I could. Better than he thought. "I used to lie awake nights, hating my father for leaving us," I told Danny. "I know it's not the same. . . ."

Danny took me in his arms as he spoke and pressed me close to his chest. "I'm sure the feelings are the same, Jess." And then he cupped my chin in his hand and tilted up my head. Our lips met, and he kissed me gently. At that moment I wished the summer would never end.

One morning after breakfast Cami and I were splashing in the pool. Danny had been handing towels out for the hotel guests, but I realized I hadn't seen him in a little while. I figured he must have run out of fresh towels and gone back for more, so I had started doing some laps when suddenly I heard him call my name.

"Jess!"

Danny was kneeling by the pool. "Great news," he said, glowing.

Janie was standing behind him, all dressed in her pastel working attire. I pulled myself out of the pool, and Danny handed me a towel to dry off. "Janie found Scott and Lila—and my father!" I had never seen Danny so happy.

"Where were they?" asked Cami, who'd just hoisted herself out of the pool.

Janie explained. "The younger two were in

foster homes not far from here. Mr. Jordan is in Maryland. . . ." Then she hesitated.

"It's okay, Ms. Baxter," Danny said. "Jess and Cami know everything. My dad's in a rehab center."

"I'm really sorry, Danny," I said sincerely.

"No, it's a good thing," he contradicted. "Thanks to your, uh, thanks to Ms. Baxter, we have a real chance of getting back together. She's going to try and find him a good job and a home. If it works, he can get custody of all of us."

I jumped up, throwing the towel off my shoulders. "Danny! That's great. It's everything you ever wanted." As I hugged him I couldn't help the little tiny sinking feeling from invading my stomach. Janie was making great progress bringing Danny's family back together. Fast progress. Which meant the end of . . . well, the end of whatever we had was also approaching.

I felt selfish for thinking about that and hugged Danny even tighter. The glow on his face said it all. All his dreams were coming true. Then I looked at Janie. I really did have to hand it to her. The stuff she was accomplishing was amazing. I still didn't like her clothes or her hair, and I'd probably never be thrilled that my dad left my mom for her. But I did have new respect for Janie now. We weren't anything alike at all; my dad had been wrong about that. But he had been right about one thing—Janie was smart. And no matter what happened, I'd never forget how hard she was working to help Danny.

Even if it turned out that helping him would separate us forever.

I tried to block that out and just continue to make the most of our time together, there at Golden's. Every once in a while I'd think about South Beach, about school, even about Jeremy Baer, who seemed like a silly crush to me now. I thought about the way I'd kissed those dumb sunglasses, still sitting on my bureau at home, and I felt like an idiot. I'd grown up so much since then.

# TWENTY

EVEN THOUGH JANIE had found Danny's dad and located Scott and Lila, there was still work to do before they could have a family reunion. Mr. Jordan had to complete his rehab, which meant he had to stay in Maryland another few weeks. During that time Janie was working on finding him a job. I felt like Danny and I had been granted a stay of execution: He was anxious to start his new life, but we both knew it would be bittersweet. His new life meant the end of our new beginning. And that was the one thing we never talked about.

Instead we spent every possible moment together, sometimes with Cami and Quentin, sometimes by ourselves. On his nights off, Danny and I often wandered out to the gazebo. He'd bring his guitar and show me some songs he was working on. Danny was self-taught, and I might have been biased, but he sounded pretty good.

175

"Is that what you want?" I'd asked him one night. "To be a musician?"

Danny sighed. "You know, Jess, I've been so focused on just getting Lisa safe and getting us out of Beaverkill. I really haven't even thought much about life beyond that."

Life beyond that . . . no, I wasn't going there either. I just removed his guitar from his shoulder and moved into his arms.

Janie's case against Lythcott was moving quickly. Because of the seriousness of the allegations and probably the dearth of big-time cases up in Beaverkill, his was moved to the top of the court's schedule. When it all started, Janie, Danny, and Lisa only had to go to the county courthouse once in a while for depositions and statements. But as July turned into August and we got closer to the end of the summer, those court visits became more frequent. Janie didn't feel comfortable discussing the case with me and Cami, but Danny let on that there were other kids in the juvenile facility ready to come forward and testify against Lythcott. I didn't know much about law beyond the shows I watched on TV, but I could tell things were going well.

In fact, the week before Labor Day, Janie burst into our room in the front of the bungalow. It was late morning, and Cami and I had been giving each other pedicures. We were surprised to see Janie still in her bathrobe. So unlike Ms. Perfect! I would have said that derisively only a month ago; now I said it to myself with new acceptance. She was human after all.

She was also out of breath as she announced, "Lythcott was indicted today! We got him on charges of harassment and endangering the welfare of a minor placed in his care. The trial starts in two weeks, and I don't think we're going to have any problem getting a conviction."

"Excellent!" Cami shouted. "That dirtbag deserves to be put away for a long time."

"That's incredible, Janie," I added. "Does Danny know?"

"Not yet. Why don't you go tell him?" Just then we heard a phone ring. It wasn't the one in our room.

"It's my cellular," Janie announced, and went back to her room to get it. She closed the door after her.

The Friday of Labor Day weekend we got a call from my dad. He was coming up so we could be together for the holiday, the last one of summer.

"I told Janie to make a reservation at the best restaurant she can find in the area." My dad chuckled. "I know it won't be anything like South Beach, but it'll have to do. We have a big announcement, and we'd like to celebrate someplace nice. Of course, Cami's invited—and so is Danny," he added. "In fact, it's important for Danny to be there because I have a feeling Janie has something awfully special to tell him."

Of course I knew what that was. No doubt Janie had arranged for Danny's father to get a job and for the family to be together. It upset me that I couldn't just feel happy for Danny without feeling all empty inside at the same time. What kind of person was I? If I truly loved Danny, I should have been joyful for him. All his dreams were about to come true. And what's that poem about when you love someone, you have to let them go . . . ?

"That's a crock," Cami declared when I asked how that poem went. "When you love someone, and he loves you . . . you hold on, you never let go!"

"Cami, is that an actual tinge of regret I hear in your voice?"

"I can't help it, Jess," she admitted, a mournful and slightly sheepish look on her face. "I'm really going to miss Quentin."

I shook my head. "I can't believe it. Camryn Welch, the human butterfly, who flits from guy to guy faster than you can blink an eye? What happened to living in the moment?"

Cami shrugged. "I guess some moments are better than others."

And some, even when they last a whole summer, seem shorter than others.

Janie had made a reservation at Abe's Steak House. "It was the best I could do," she acknowledged. "There wasn't much choice in the area."

It was fine. I mean, I'd actually grown to like the Rellecks and their friends, but a meal without them anywhere nearby, was a relief. I settled into a booth next to Danny. Cami sat on his other side, my dad and Janie across from us. As soon as the waiter took our order my dad said, "First, Janie and I have an announcement. We've chosen a date for our wedding."

"I'd be especially honored, Jess, if you would be my maid of honor," Janie said, smiling over at me.

Without a second thought I said, "I'll be there, Janie."

Then she turned to Cami. "We'd be delighted if you would be there, Cami . . . but maybe you could think about wearing something a little toned down, dear?"

I laughed. "Don't worry, I'll take her shopping."

"This calls for a toast," Danny broke in, raising his water glass. "To the two of you . . . the future Mr. and Mrs. Graham."

"Actually, Danny," Janie corrected him, "it's going to be Baxter–Graham. Or Graham–Baxter. We haven't decided yet."

My dad and Janie were beaming. They looked so happy together, I couldn't help but smile. I squeezed Danny's arm, suddenly feeling a rush of sadness. In two days I would get on a plane for Miami. I'd be going home, and who knew when I'd ever see him again? I couldn't imagine life going on without him. Was I supposed to just go back to school on Tuesday morning and pretend the whole summer hadn't even happened?

Janie cleared her throat. "And then there's another announcement I have." She looked straight at Danny.

"I found your father a job." Before anyone could react, Janie rushed on. "I've spoken to him several times over the past few weeks. He's had a lot of tough breaks in his life, but he's a good man, Danny."

Danny smiled. "Yeah, I've always known that."

"He can't wait to get all you kids back together and his life back on track. We talked about the kind of job he'd be qualified for, and we settled on construction."

"That makes sense," Danny mused. "That's what he used to do before . . . well, before everything fell apart."

*Just like everything between us is about to fall apart,* I thought mournfully.

I was feeling so sorry for myself, I barely heard what Janie was saying. Suddenly, like a pure white beam of light, her words pierced through my fog of self-pity.

"Through my contacts I was able to get him placed with the Dade County Development Project."

My jaw fell open. "Dade County?" I repeated in astonishment. "You mean Dade County in Florida?"

Danny turned to me. "Is that close to South Beach?"

"South Beach is *in* Dade County," I said breathlessly, my eyes brimming with tears. I suddenly knew that Janie hadn't been looking for just any job that would get Mr. Jordan and his family back together. She'd taken all that extra time to find one near me.

"That's right," Janie was saying. "There happen to be some very good job opportunities down there these days. I knew a few people in that business when I was working down there, so I pulled some strings. It shouldn't be hard to find an apartment big enough for your whole family, and there are lots of good schools for Lisa, Lila, and Scott. As for you, Danny—well, I don't see why you couldn't finish up your last year at South Beach High."

I couldn't believe it. I threw my arms around Danny.

Danny was still bewildered. "Jessie, that's near you, right?"

"Danny, South Beach High is my school!"

A huge grin spread across his face. "Really?"

I nodded. "Really."

Danny grabbed my hand. "Come on, I want to show you something outside." As Cami got up so we could squeeze out of the booth, Danny turned to Janie. "I–I don't know quite how to thank you," he said, his voice cracking. "You really turned my life—my family's life—around."

Janie smiled. "It was my pleasure."

Danny bent down and gave Janie a quick peck on the cheek. "We'll be right back," he told my dad.

I followed Danny outside and around the back of the restaurant.

"The sun has just set," he explained. Danny

pointed upward, toward a sliver of purplish blue sky. "This is the best time to see it."

"See what?" I asked, peering up at the sky.

"Mercury!"

I couldn't be sure if Danny was just saying that or if that sliver really was Mercury. "Of course," Danny said, "we'll get a much better view of it in Florida, our first night at the beach together."

I smiled. "I can't wait."

Danny shook his head. "I thought I'd have to give you up, Jess. That I'd have to give up one dream for another to come true. I can't believe I can really have both."

"If anyone deserves complete happiness, it's you, Danny."

"And if anyone makes me completely happy, it's you, Jessica." He paused. "I'm not really sure if that's Mercury," he admitted. "So I guess I'll show you what I really brought you out here for." Danny put his arms around me and leaned down to kiss me tenderly. "Mercury was just an excuse for that."

I gazed into his beautiful brown eyes. As always, they seemed to have a special message just for me. But this time the words came from his lips as well.

"I love you, Jess," he said softly.

*Do you ever wonder about falling in love? About members of the opposite sex? Do you need a little friendly advice but have no one to turn to? Well, that's where we come in . . . Jenny and Jake. Send us those questions you're dying to ask, and we'll give you the straight scoop on life and love in the nineties.*

## DEAR JAKE

**Q:** *My problem is my best friend. She's really pretty and friendly, so guys always like her and never even notice me. I don't know how to find someone who will actually want me instead of my friend. Plus I wish I could tell her not to go out with the guys I like, but I don't want to make her mad at me. What can I do to break out of her shadow?*

**LD, Columbia, MD**

**A:** It must be rough to have a good friend who gets all the attention when you're too shy to ask for any of it yourself. My guess is that you have just as much to offer as your friend does, but you're so down on yourself that you don't give anyone the chance to show interest in you. Try finding ways to feel better about yourself, like making a mental list of everything you have going for you. Trust me, when you start acting like you're worth it, guys will be attracted to your confidence.

As for your friend, you have to tell her that what she's doing is hurting you if you want her to stop. Let her know that you care about her friendship and you want her to be happy. But you also wish that she would back off the guys you're interested in and give you some space to show off the new, confident you. If she's a true friend, she'll support you and understand without getting angry.

Q: *Ever since my boyfriend broke up with me, I've been spending more time with my guy friends. Now he's flirting with me again, and he keeps asking me out. I care about him, but I need to know if he really wants me back or if he's just jealous that I'm spending so much time with other guys.*

*KR, Exeter, CA*

A: Jealousy is one of the most powerful drives for myself and my fellow guys. We can't *stand* to see you with other guys. You're certainly right to wonder if this is what's motivating your ex-boyfriend's sudden renewed interest in you.

In order to find out if he's for real, take a little time away from your guy friends and see if your ex still goes after you. If he's really serious about being with you and you still want to go out with him, make it clear that your friends will still be a part of your life but your heart is definitely his.

# DEAR JENNY

**Q:** *I'm in a really confusing situation. I'm dating a guy named Corey who is two inches shorter than I am, and sometimes I worry that people will laugh at me. I'm also afraid that I'll accidentally say something about his height and hurt his feelings. I like Corey, but I don't know if I can deal with dating a short guy. What should I do?*

**BX, Myrtle Beach, SC**

**A:** It's tough to date someone shorter than you when you're used to looking *up* into your boyfriend's eyes. There are definitely people out there who might tease you about the height difference, but anyone who would make fun of something so silly isn't worth your time, anyway. You wouldn't let other people tell you who to date, so why let their shallow opinions influence you?

Guys are often embarrassed about being short, and your boyfriend is probably more upset about his height than you are, so you should be careful not to say anything that would hurt him. It sounds like you really need to decide how much this guy means to you. If you really like him, then it shouldn't matter how tall he is. But if this is a big problem for you, you can't stay with someone you're not comfortable dating.

**Q:** *I have been best friends with Luke since we were seven years old. We have always gone to dances, parties, and concerts together. I've even slept over at his house! Now we're sixteen, and Luke* *wants to be my boyfriend. The problem is that when he kissed me, it felt like I was kissing my brother. Luke still wants more than a friendship, but I don't. If I say no, will I lose my best friend?*

*HW, Dunedin, New Zealand*

**A:** Friendships with guys can be a lot of fun, and it sounds like what you have with Luke is really special. However, you've just discovered the biggest problem with guy buddies. When one friend wants more than the other, it's difficult to keep feelings from getting hurt.

The first thing you have to do is be honest with Luke. If you know this can't be more than a friendship, tell him. Make sure that he understands how much he means to you but explain that you've known him too long to see him as anything other than your best friend. Be prepared for the fact that Luke might need some time alone to nurse his broken heart. Hopefully it won't take him too long to realize how much he needs your friendship.

*Do you have questions about love? Write to:*

Jenny Burgess or Jake Korman
c/o Daniel Weiss Associates
33 West 17th Street
New York, NY 10011